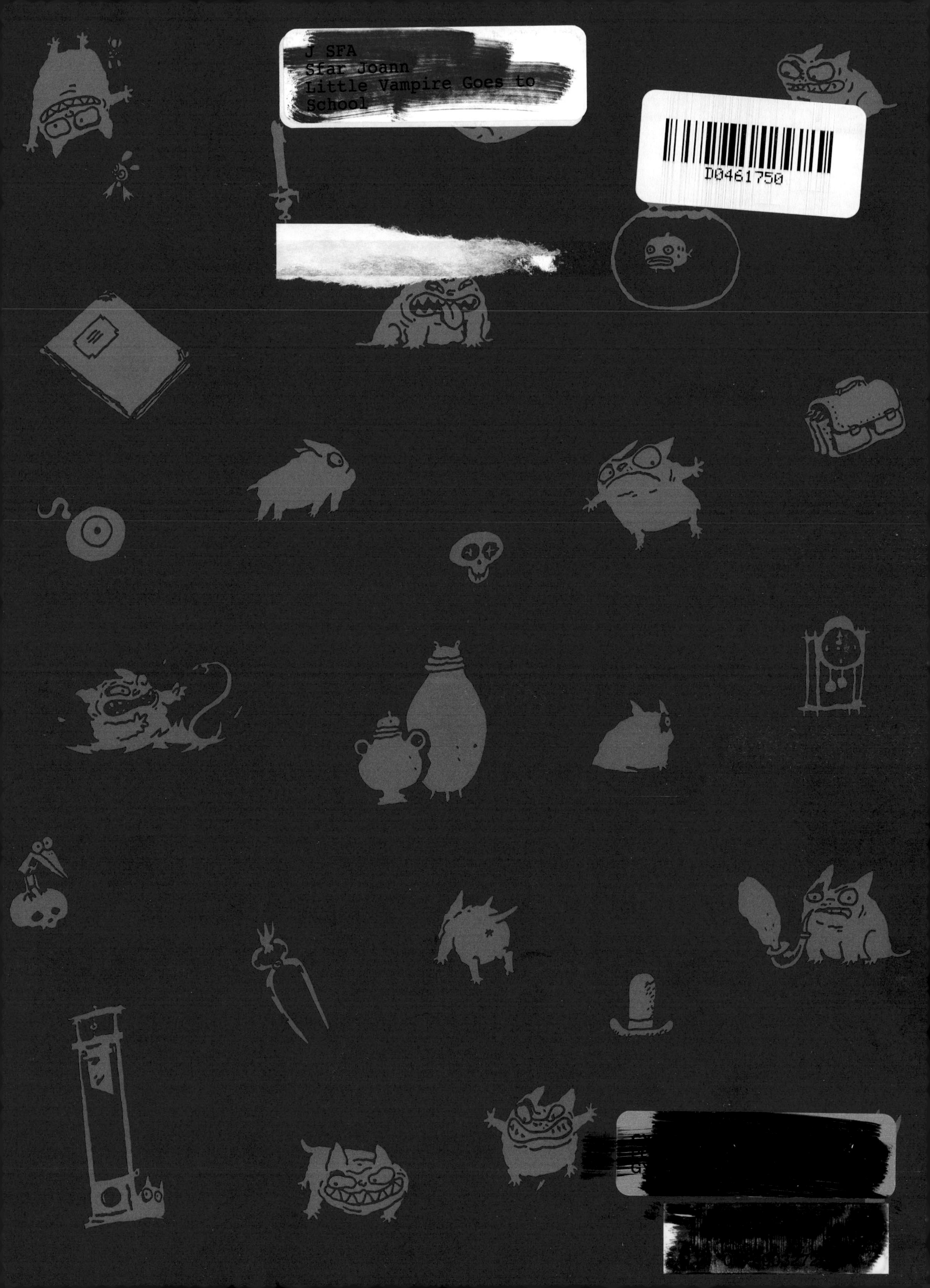

LITTLE VAMPIRE

GOES TO SCHOOL

Stories and drawings by
Joann Sfar

Colors by
Walter

Simon & Schuster Books for Young Readers
New York   London   Toronto   Sydney   Singapore

SIMON & SCHUSTER BOOKS FOR YOUNG READERS
An imprint of Simon & Schuster Children's Publishing Division
1230 Avenue of the Americas, New York, New York 10020

Originally published in France in 1999 as *Petit Vampire va à l'école* by Guy Delcourt
Productions

Translated by Mark and Alexis Siegel
Book design by Mark Siegel
The text for this book is set in Printhouse and Wendy.
The illustrations for this book are rendered in ink and digital color.

Manufactured in France
10 9 8 7 6 5 4 3 2 1
CIP data for this book is available from the Library of Congress.
ISBN 0-689-85717-9

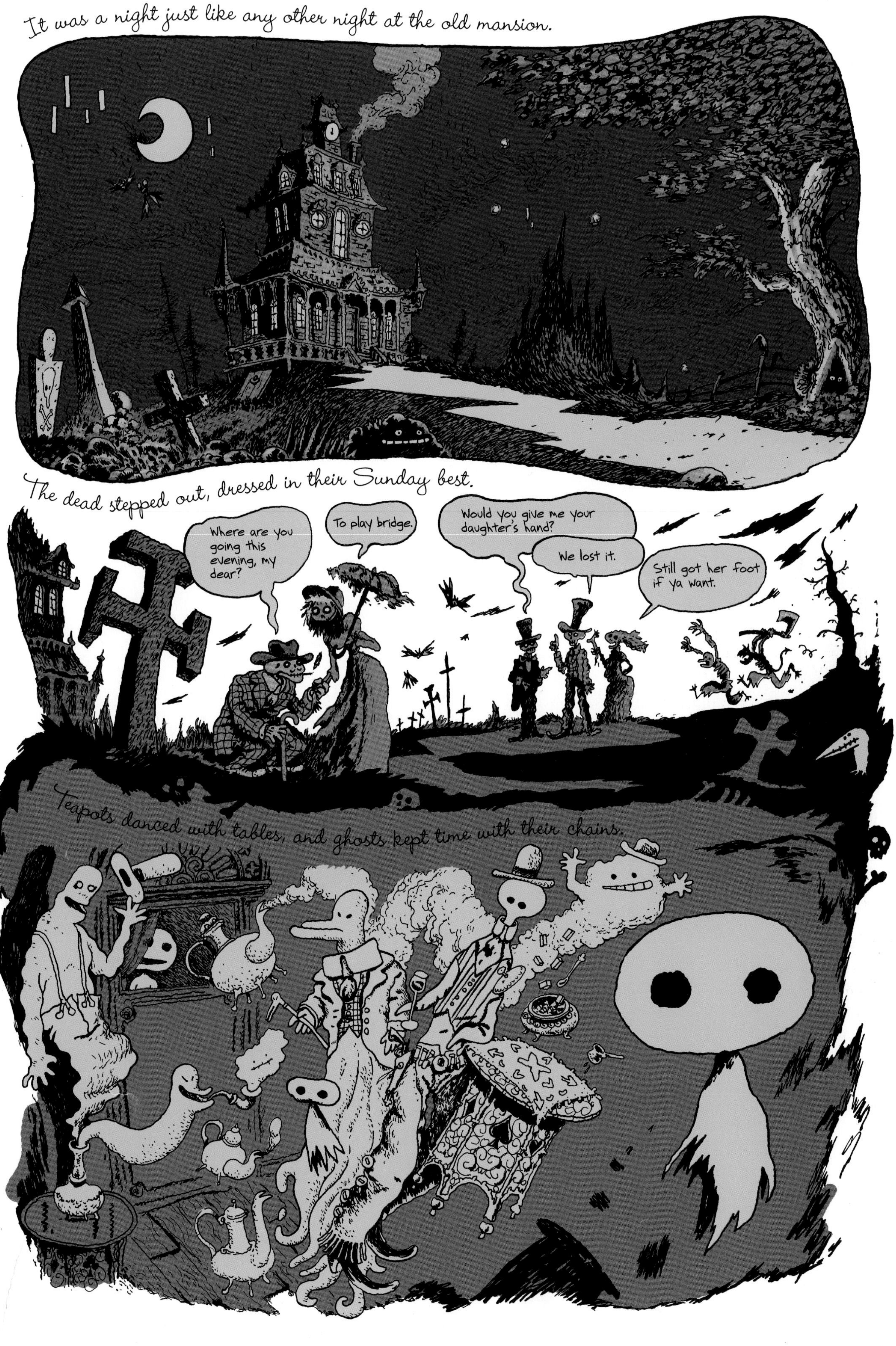
It was a night just like any other night at the old mansion.
The dead stepped out, dressed in their Sunday best.
Where are you going this evening, my dear?
To play bridge.
Would you give me your daughter's hand?
We lost it.
Still got her foot if ya want.
Teapots danced with tables, and ghosts kept time with their chains.

Ancestors slipped out of their dusty portraits to have a little fun as they did every night. All was well, and yet somebody was sad.

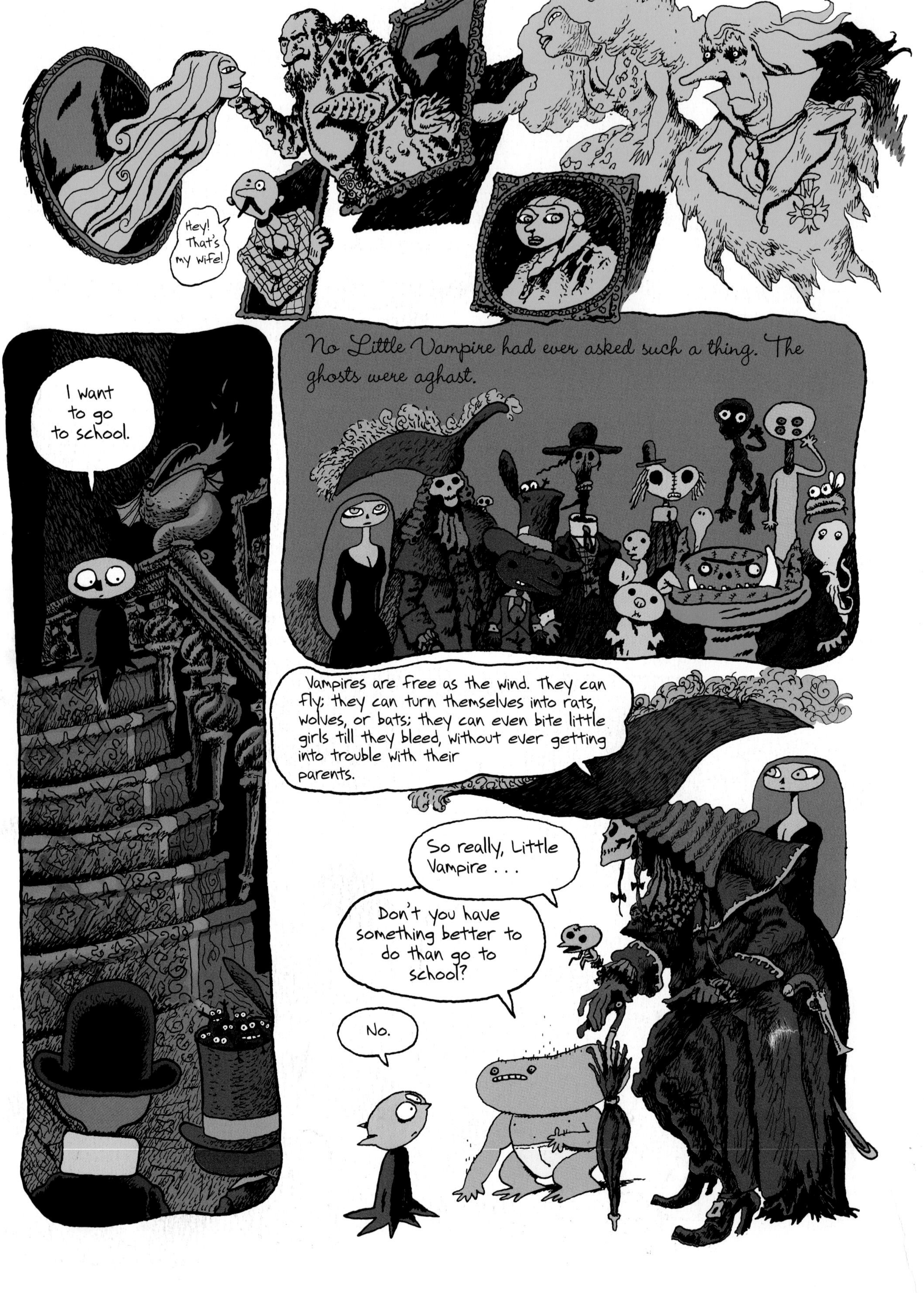
Hey! That's my wife!
I want to go to school.
No Little Vampire had ever asked such a thing. The ghosts were aghast.
Vampires are free as the wind. They can fly; they can turn themselves into rats, wolves, or bats; they can even bite little girls till they bleed, without ever getting into trouble with their parents.
So really, Little Vampire . . .
Don't you have something better to do than go to school?
No.

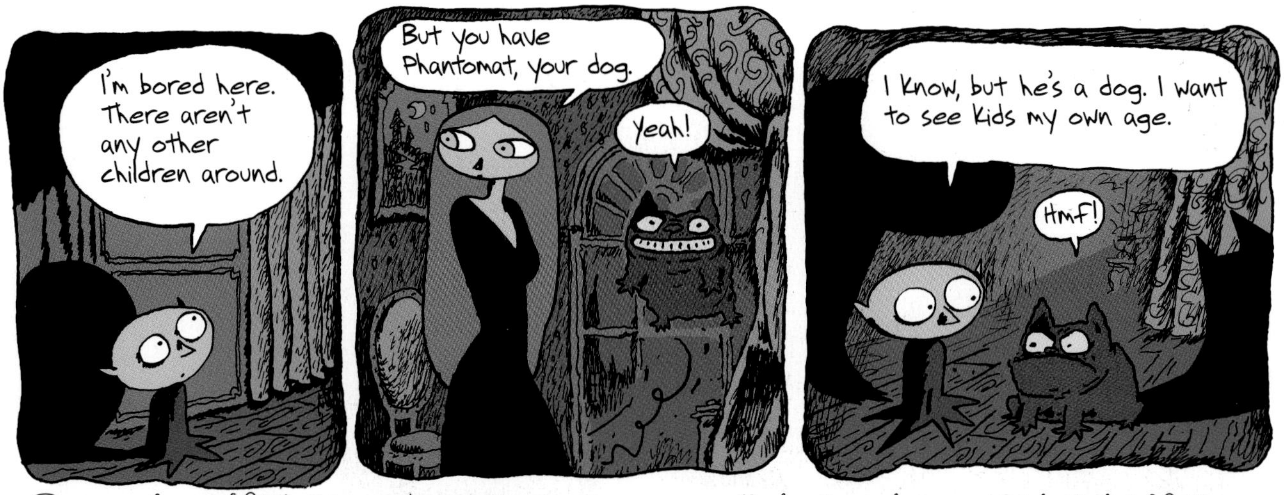
I'm bored here. There aren't any other children around.
But you have Phantomat, your dog.
Yeah!
I know, but he's a dog. I want to see kids my own age.
Hmf!

Everyone found Little Vampire's request very strange, especially his dog, who was a bit hurt that Little Vampire would prefer kids his own age over him.

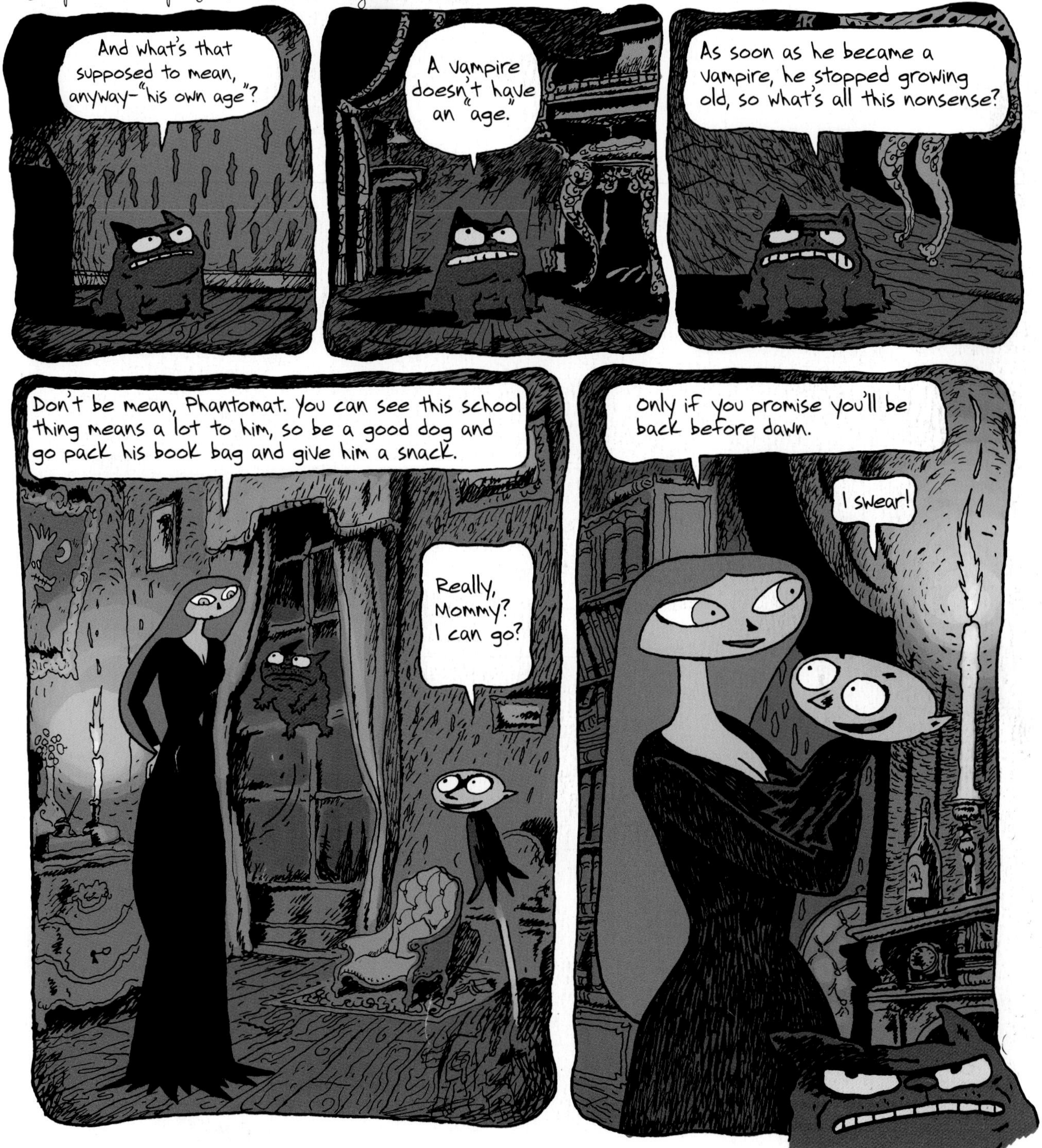
And what's that supposed to mean, anyway—"his own age"?
A vampire doesn't have an "age."
As soon as he became a vampire, he stopped growing old, so what's all this nonsense?
Don't be mean, Phantomat. You can see this school thing means a lot to him, so be a good dog and go pack his book bag and give him a snack.
Really, Mommy? I can go?
Only if you promise you'll be back before dawn.
I swear!

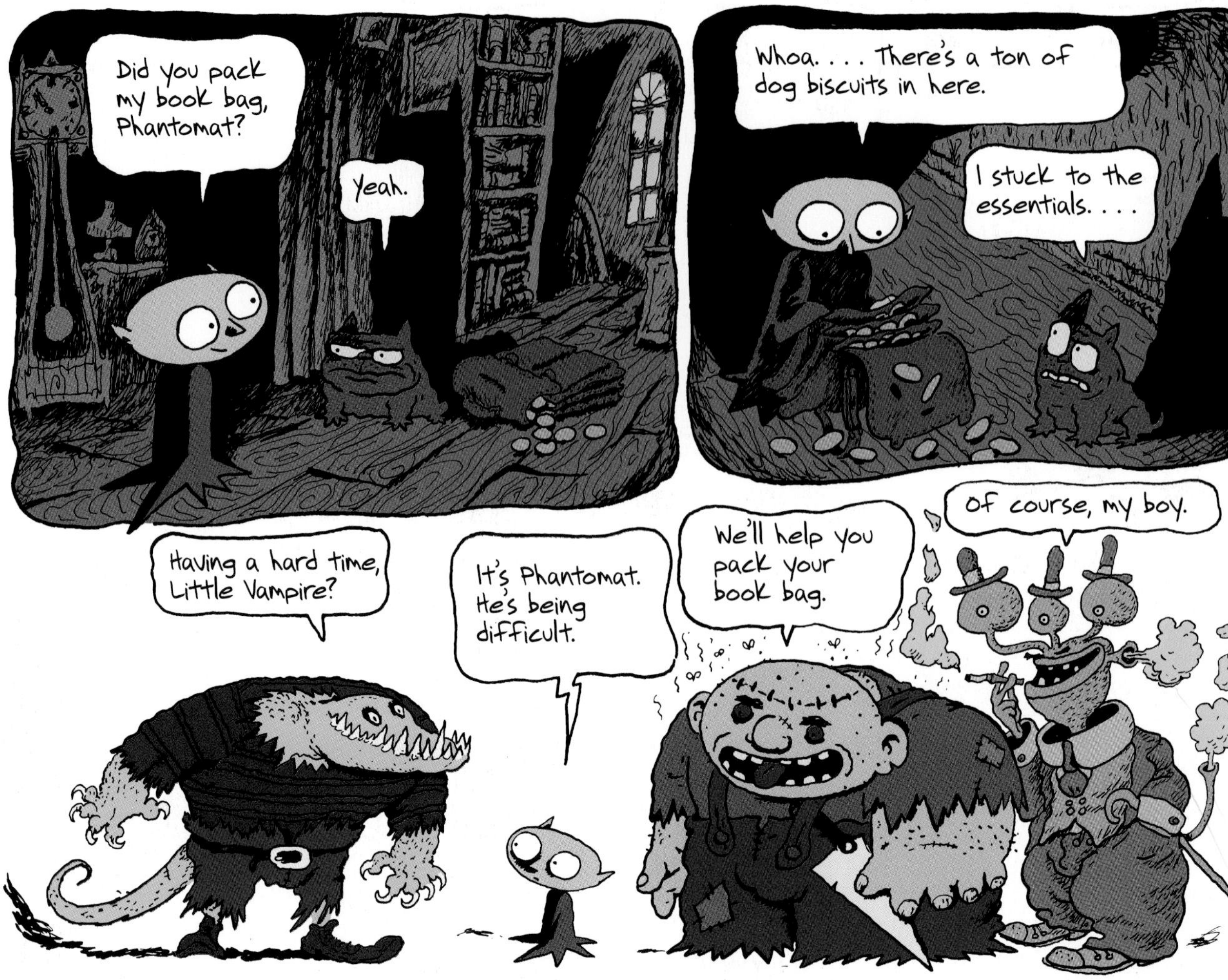
Did you pack my book bag, Phantomat?
Yeah.
Whoa. . . . There's a ton of dog biscuits in here.
I stuck to the essentials. . . .
Having a hard time, Little Vampire?
It's Phantomat. He's being difficult.
We'll help you pack your book bag.
Of course, my boy.

Monsters are helpful folk, and they very quickly began to make school supplies from odds and ends they found in the old house.

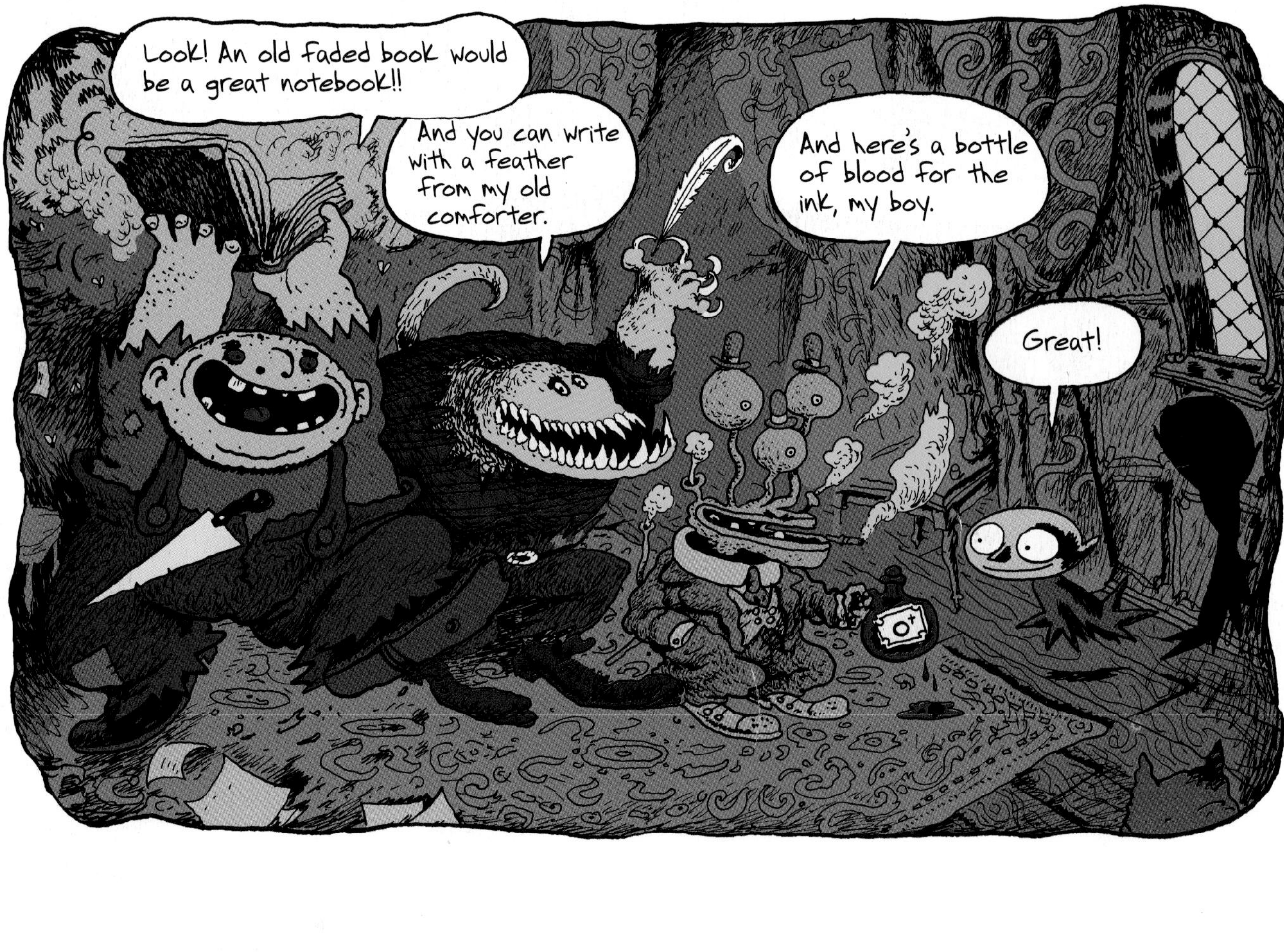
Look! An old faded book would be a great notebook!!
And you can write with a feather from my old comforter.
And here's a bottle of blood for the ink, my boy.
Great!

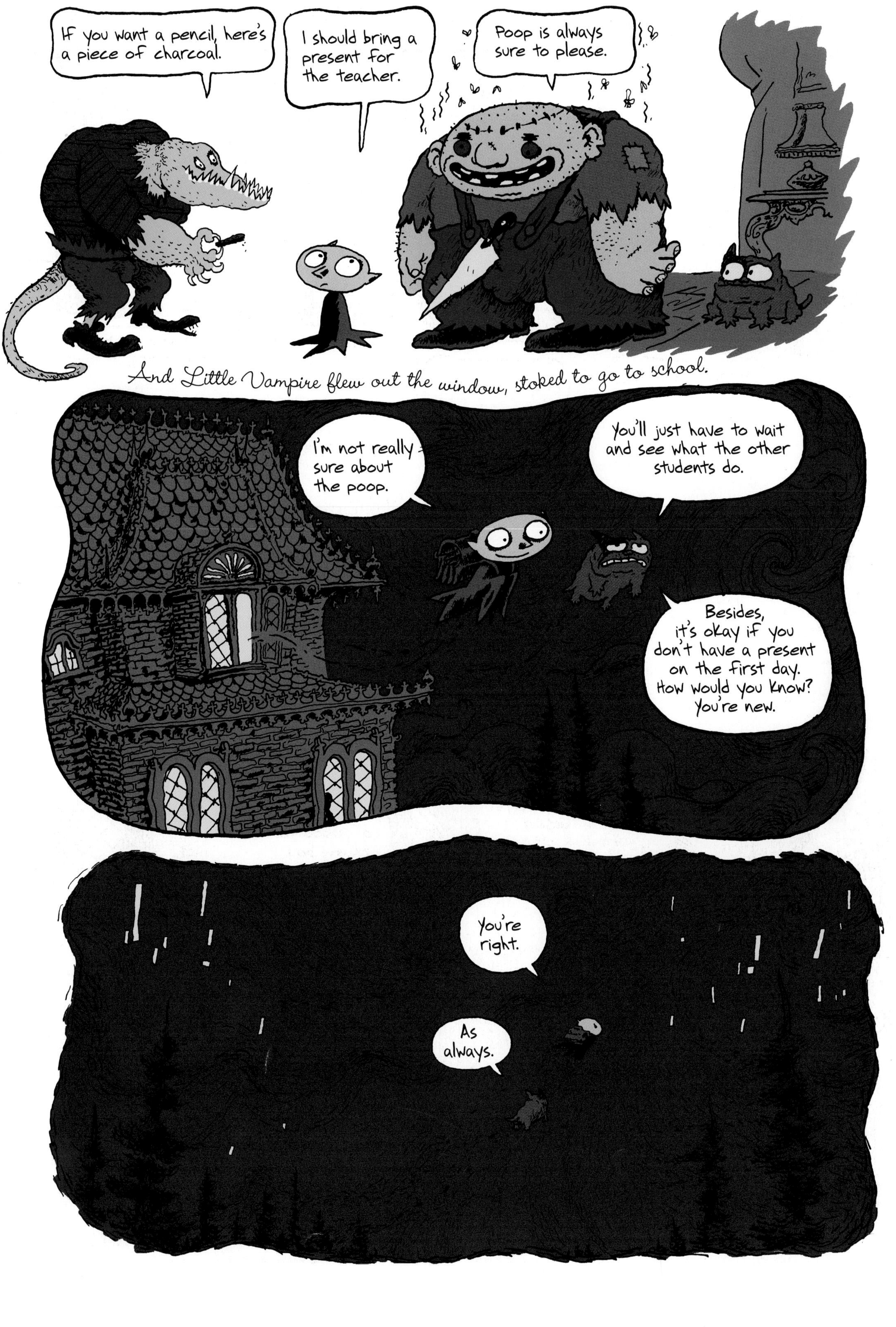
If you want a pencil, here's a piece of charcoal.
I should bring a present for the teacher.
Poop is always sure to please.
And Little Vampire flew out the window, stoked to go to school.
I'm not really sure about the poop.
You'll just have to wait and see what the other students do.
Besides, it's okay if you don't have a present on the first day. How would you know? You're new.
You're right.
As always.

It was a nice two-story school on the edge of town. There was a playground with swings, a sandbox, and an aviary full of doves.

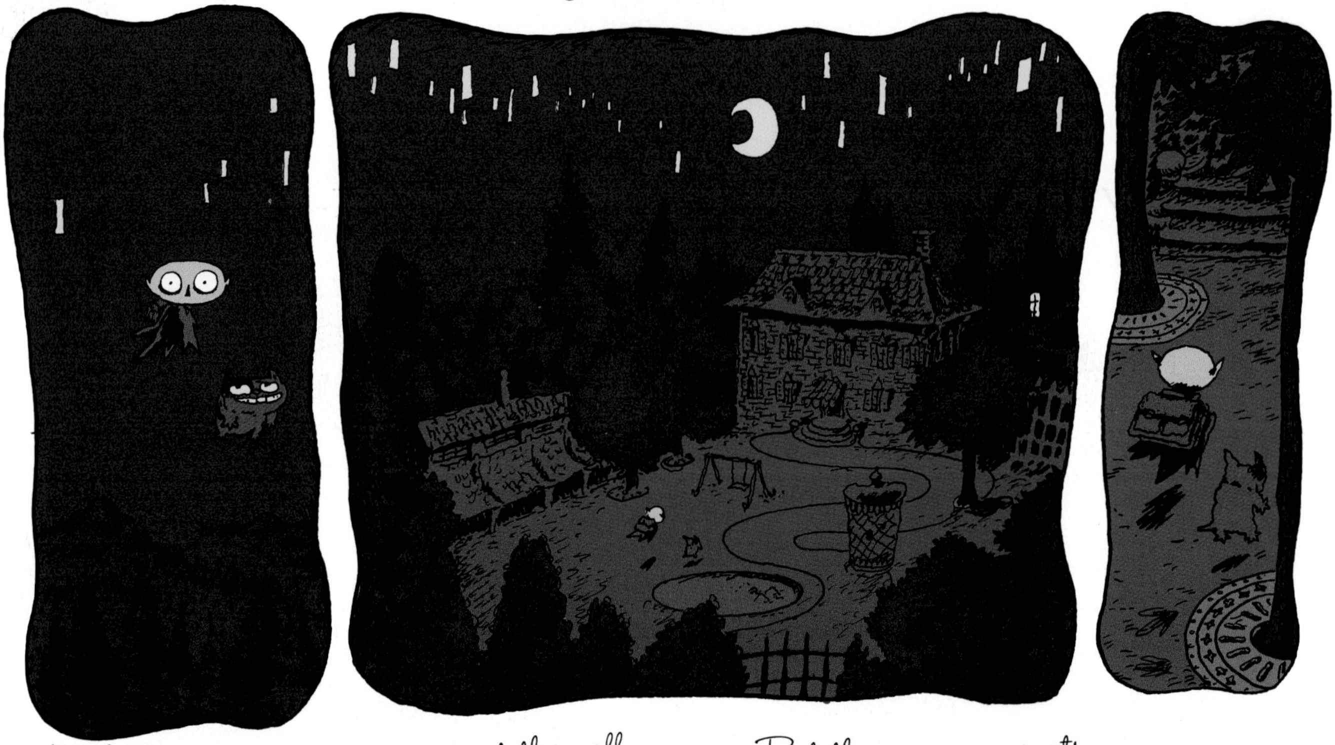

In the hallway wooden hooks lined the wall at just the right height, so students could hang their coats.

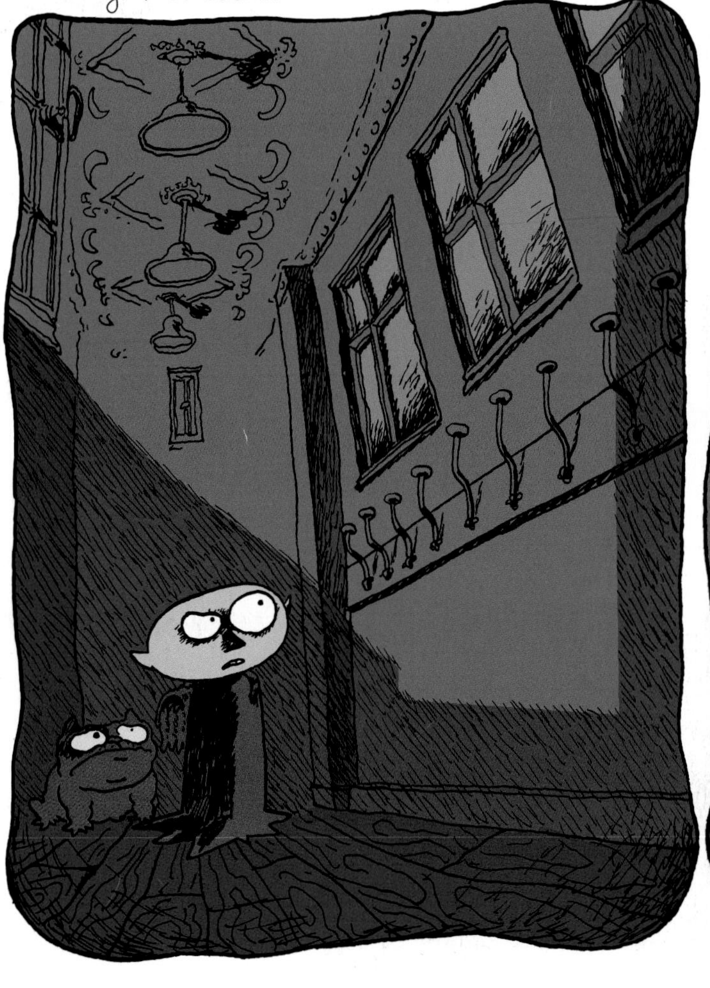

But there were no coats.

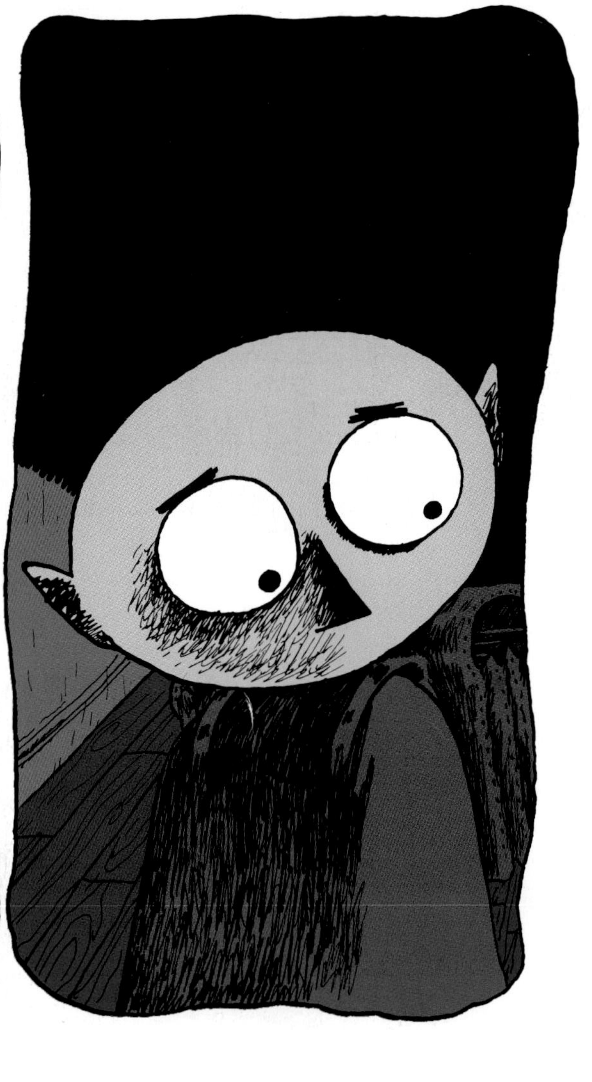

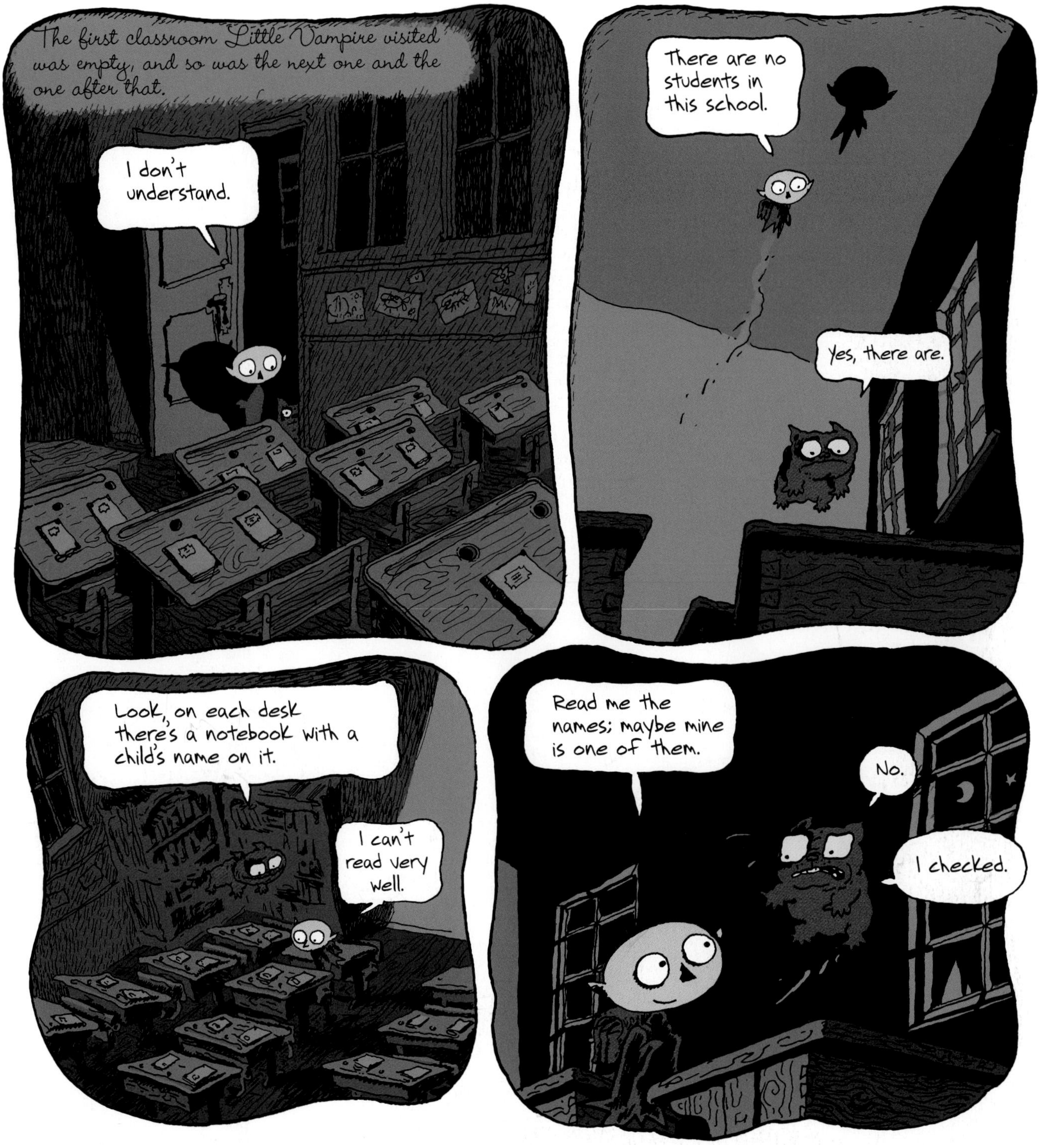
The first classroom Little Vampire visited was empty, and so was the next one and the one after that.
I don't understand.
There are no students in this school.
Yes, there are.
Look, on each desk there's a notebook with a child's name on it.
I can't read very well.
Read me the names; maybe mine is one of them.
No.
I checked.

"Maybe students only go to school in broad daylight. And at night there's nobody here."

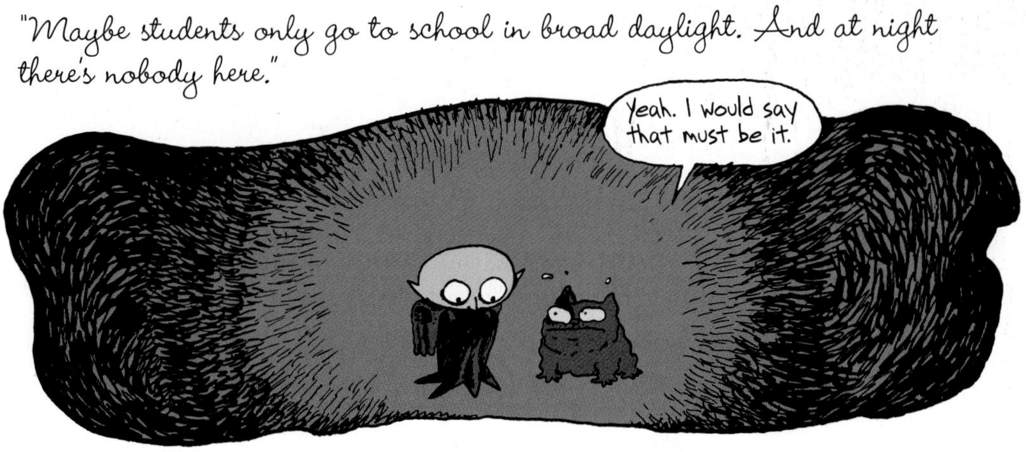
Yeah. I would say that must be it.

Little Vampire's mother had expected to see him come back at dawn, all excited about school, so she was worried when he came back early, hanging his head.

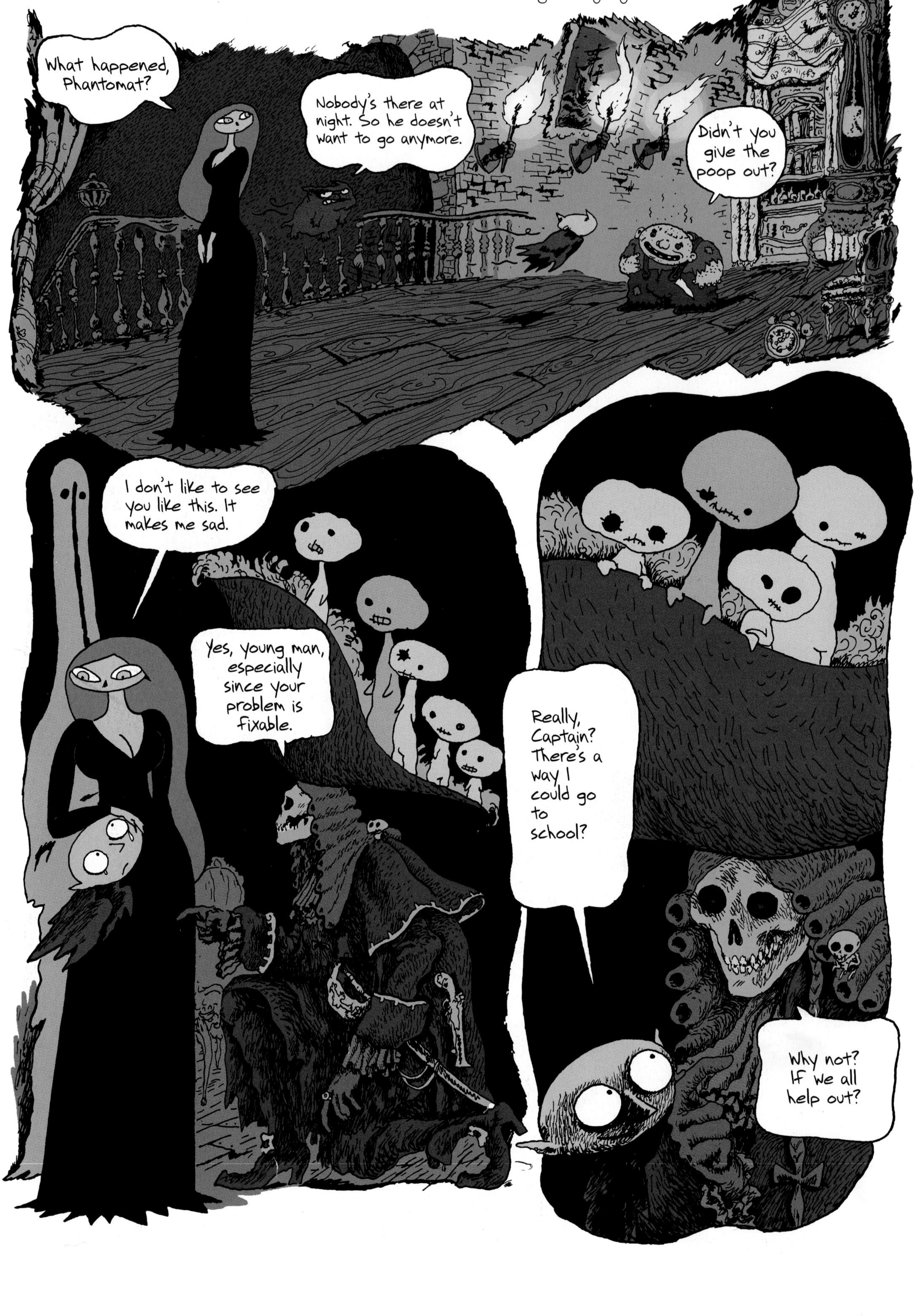
What happened, Phantomat?
Nobody's there at night. So he doesn't want to go anymore.
Didn't you give the poop out?
I don't like to see you like this. It makes me sad.
Yes, young man, especially since your problem is fixable.
Really, Captain? There's a way I could go to school?
Why not? If we all help out?

The next night, the ghosts agreed to meet at the school to make Little Vampire happy.

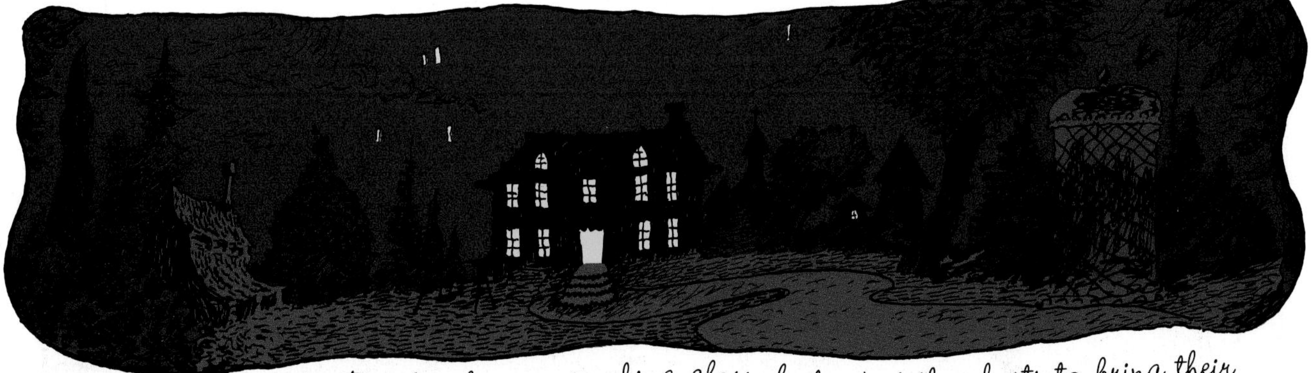

The Captain of the Dead, who was teaching class, had asked the ghosts to bring their own school supplies so they wouldn't write in any of the daytime students' notebooks.

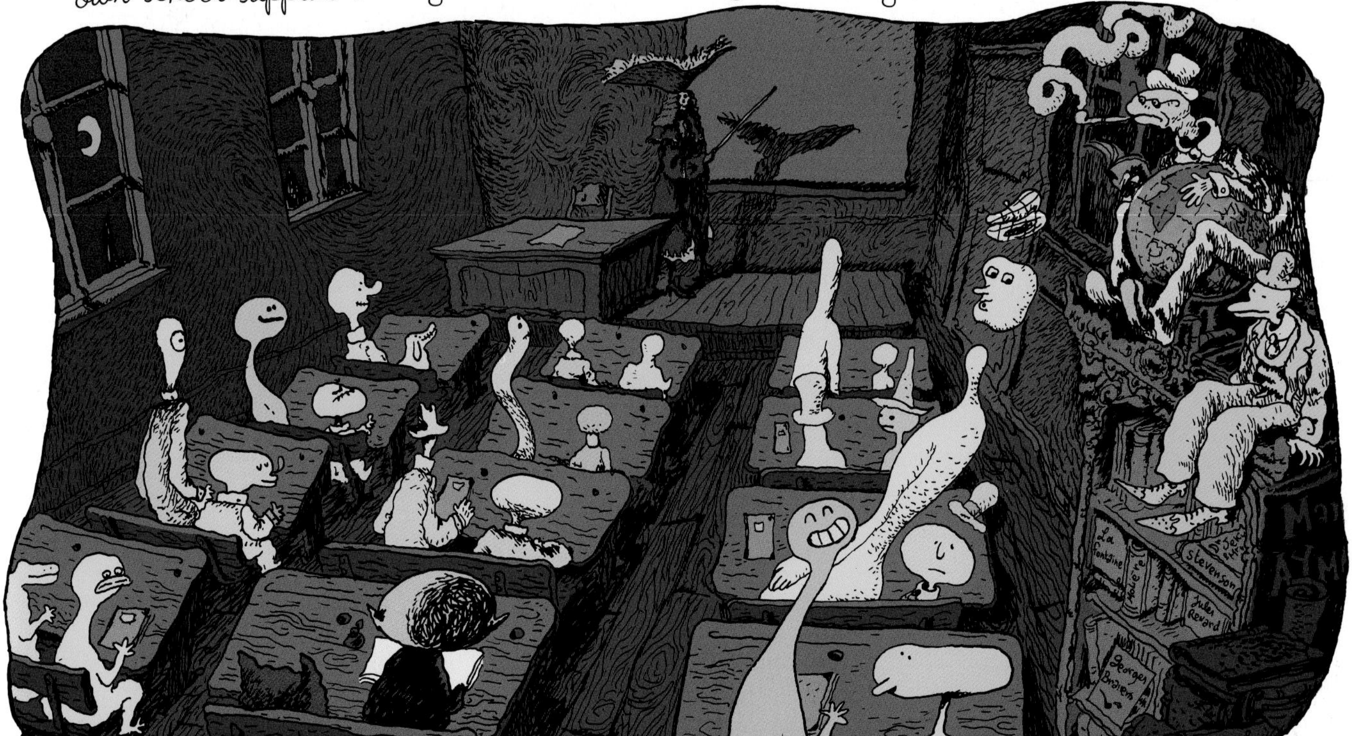

Because ghosts shouldn't be noticed by mortals.

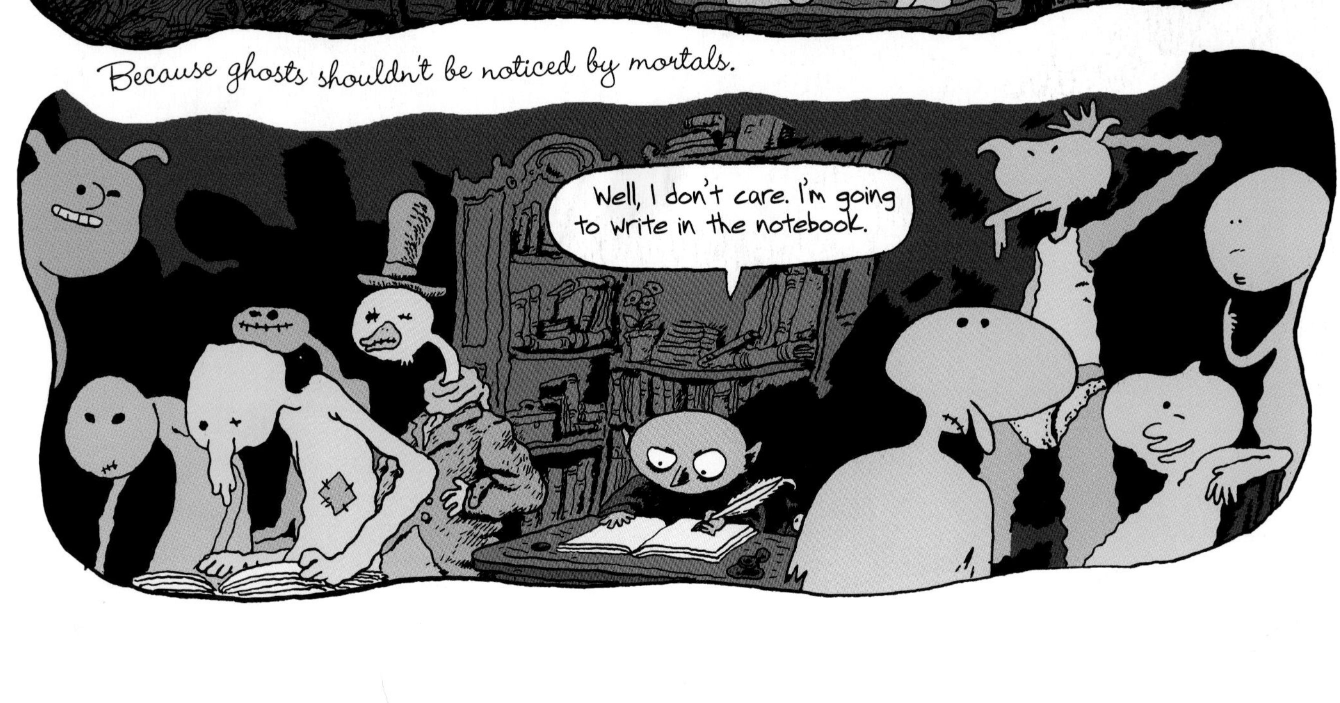
Well, I don't care. I'm going to write in the notebook.

The next day, in the same classroom, the schoolteacher quizzed her pupils: "Michael Duffin, did you do your homework?"

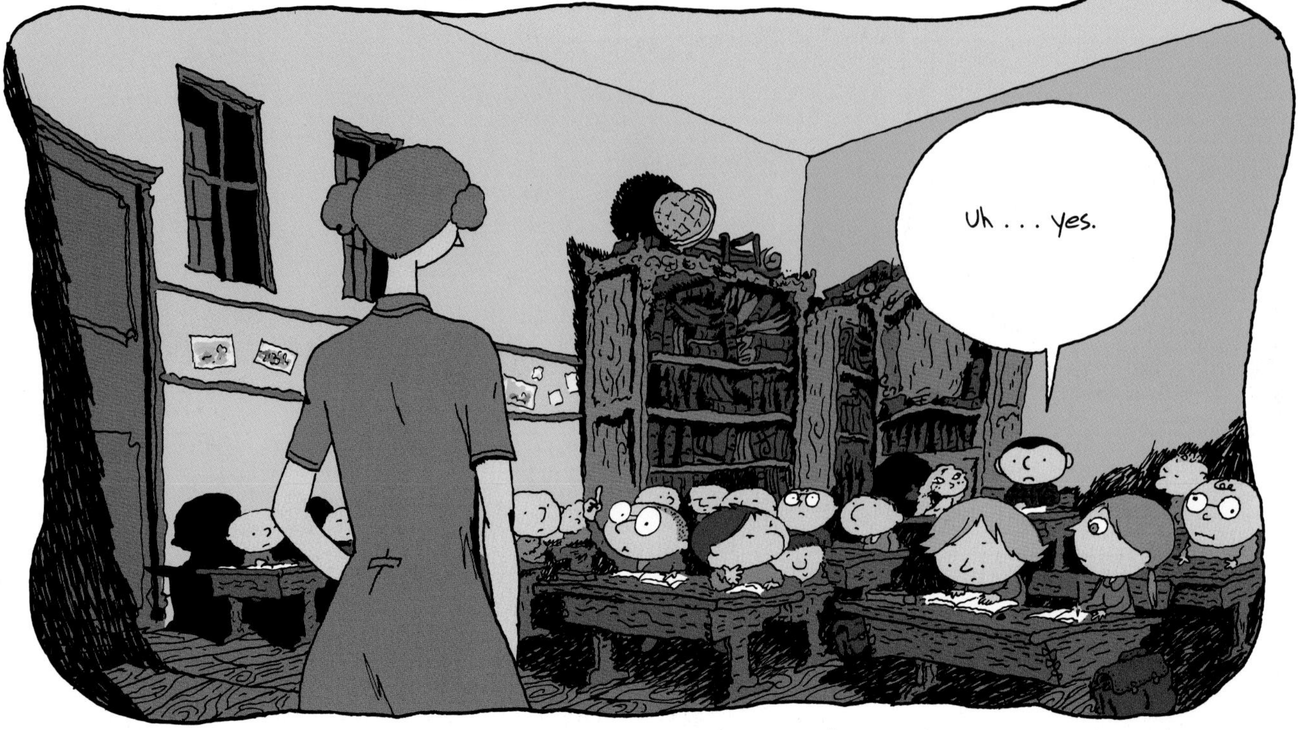
Uh . . . yes.

"Come on then, open your notebook," the schoolteacher said, "and read what you wrote." Michael opened his notebook and squirmed. Because, the truth is, he didn't do his homework.

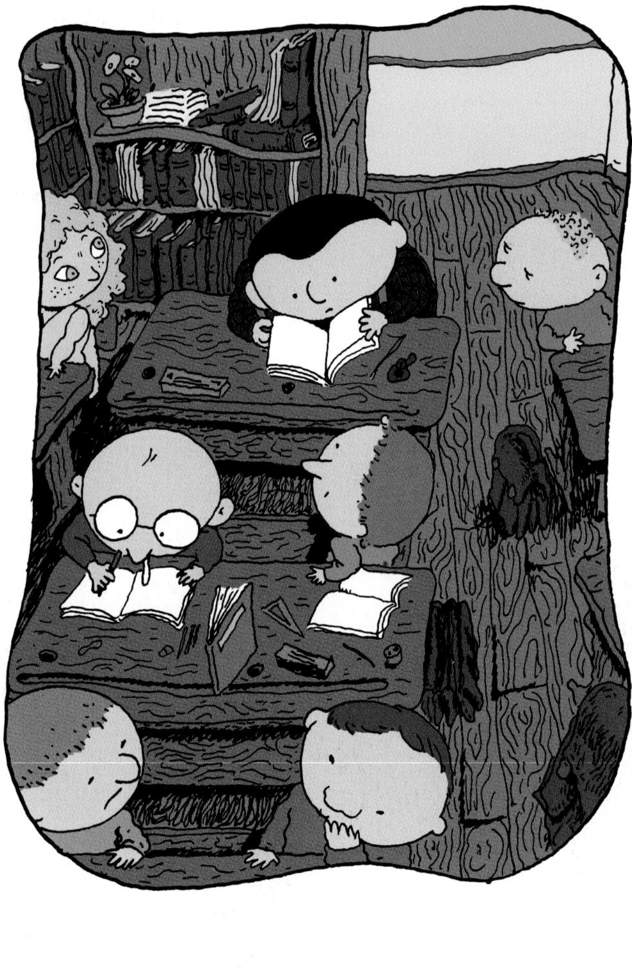

But there in his notebook, a miracle: His homework was done, and there were no mistakes!

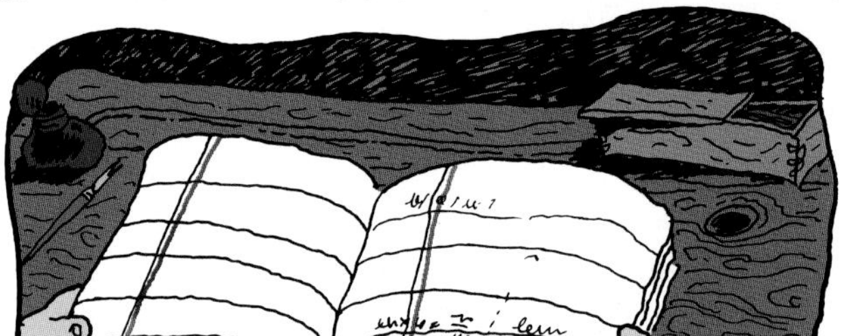

Michael couldn't believe it.

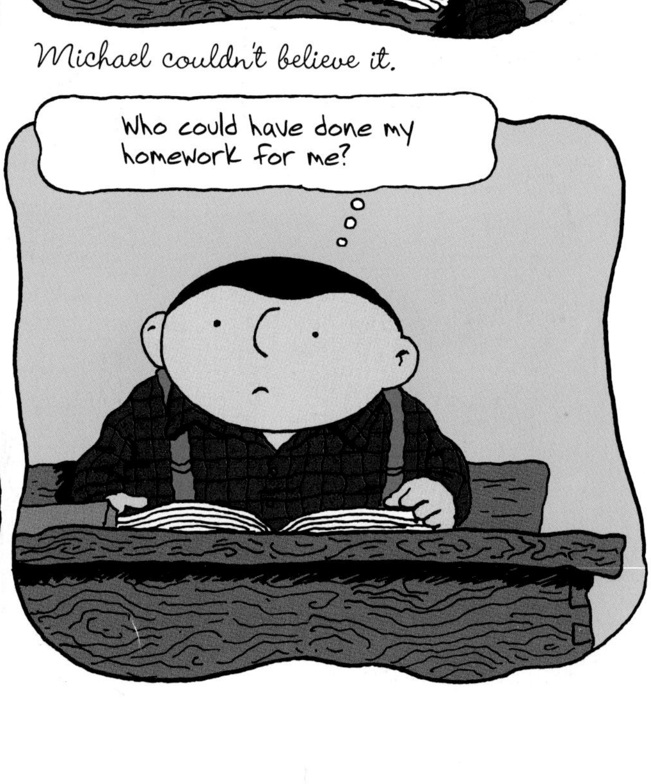
Who could have done my homework for me?

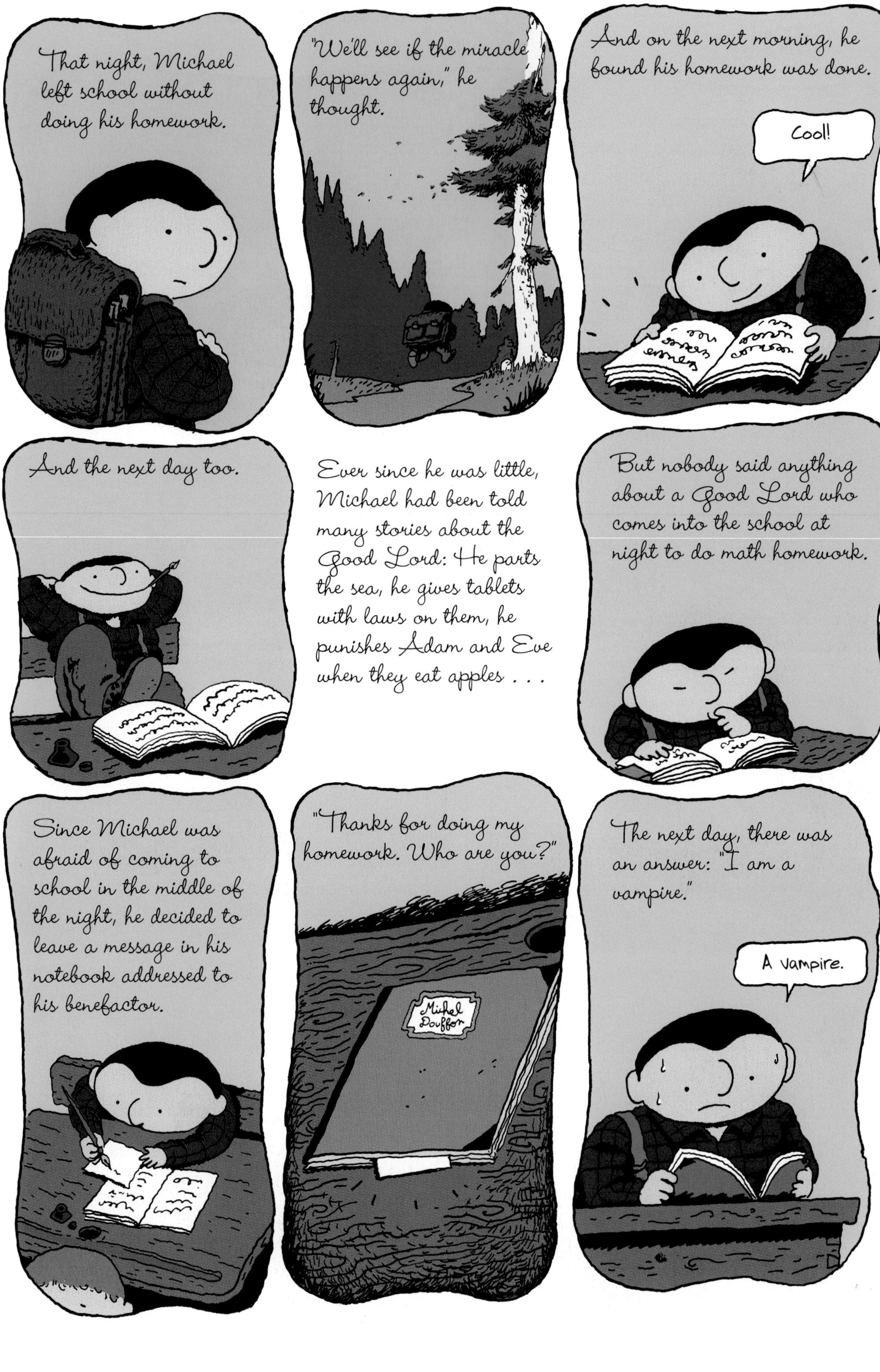
That night, Michael left school without doing his homework.
"We'll see if the miracle happens again," he thought.
And on the next morning, he found his homework was done.
Cool!
And the next day too.
Ever since he was little, Michael had been told many stories about the Good Lord: He parts the sea, he gives tablets with laws on them, he punishes Adam and Eve when they eat apples . . .
But nobody said anything about a Good Lord who comes into the school at night to do math homework.
Since Michael was afraid of coming to school in the middle of the night, he decided to leave a message in his notebook addressed to his benefactor.
"Thanks for doing my homework. Who are you?"
The next day, there was an answer: "I am a vampire."
A vampire.

From that day on, Michael and Little Vampire left notes for each other.

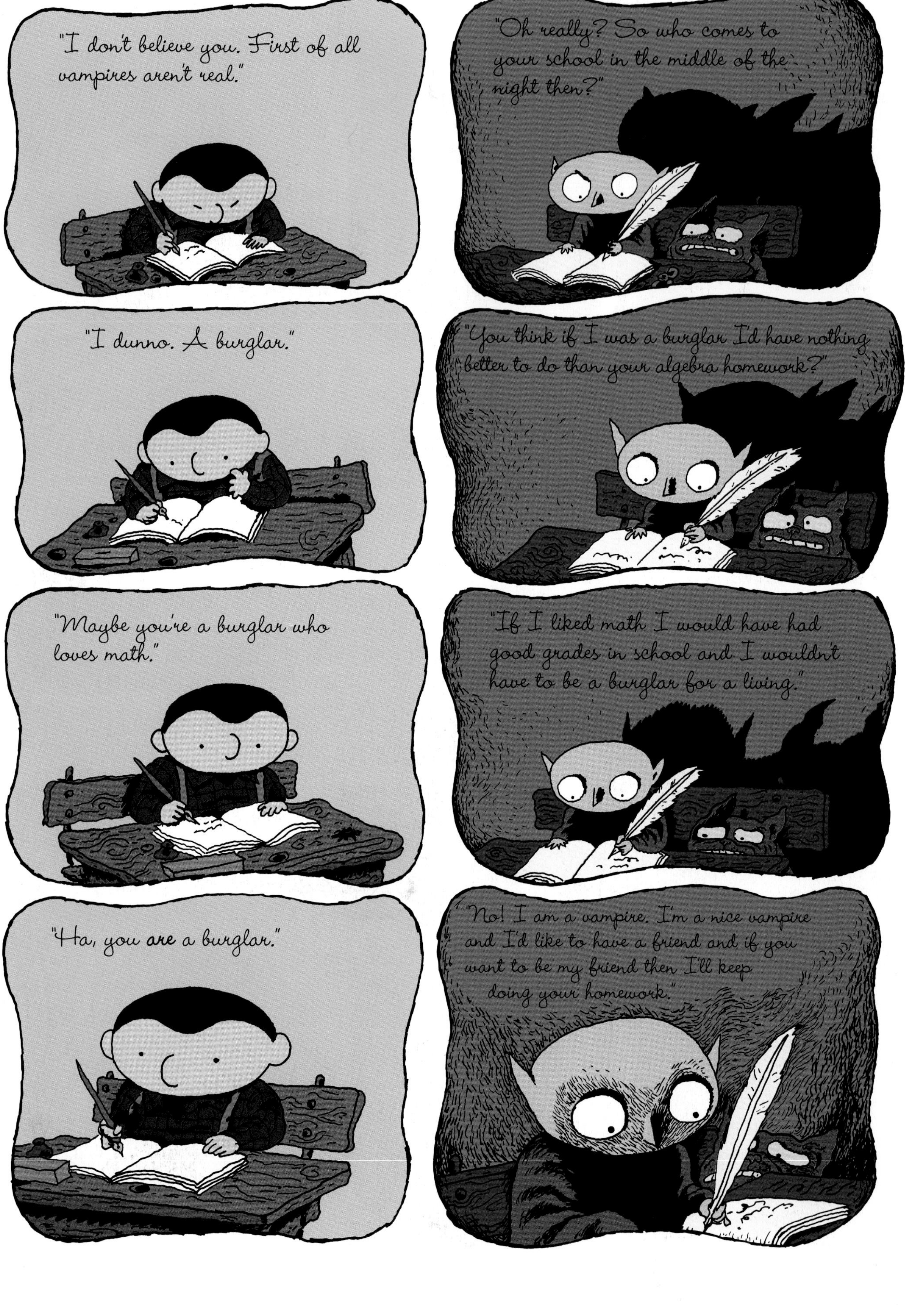
"I don't believe you. First of all vampires aren't real."
"Oh really? So who comes to your school in the middle of the night then?"
"I dunno. A burglar."
"You think if I was a burglar I'd have nothing better to do than your algebra homework?"
"Maybe you're a burglar who loves math."
"If I liked math I would have had good grades in school and I wouldn't have to be a burglar for a living."
"Ha, you **are** a burglar."
"No! I am a vampire. I'm a nice vampire and I'd like to have a friend and if you want to be my friend then I'll keep doing your homework."

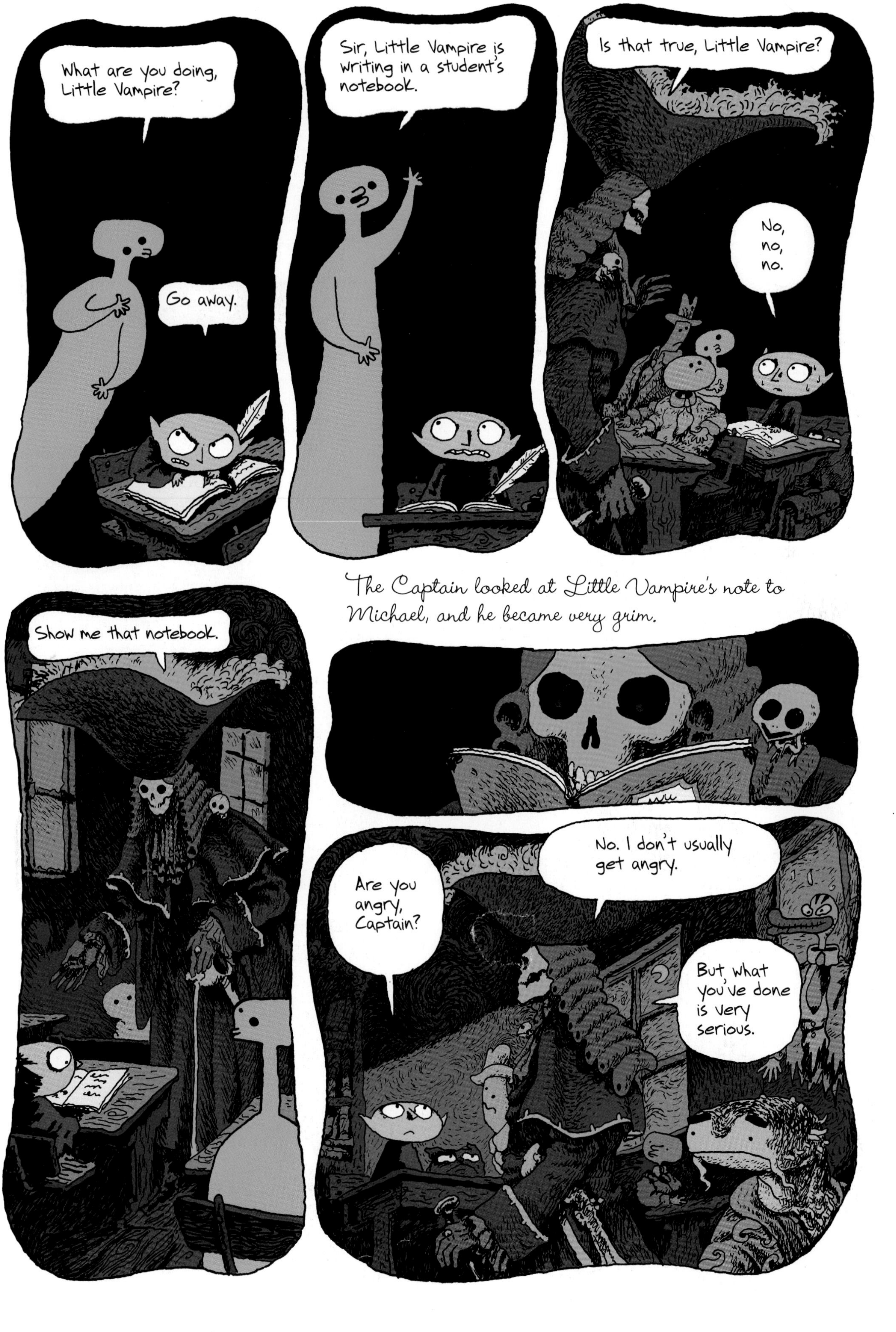

What are you doing, Little Vampire?
Go away.
Sir, Little Vampire is writing in a student's notebook.
Is that true, Little Vampire?
No, no, no.
Show me that notebook.
The Captain looked at Little Vampire's note to Michael, and he became very grim.
Are you angry, Captain?
No. I don't usually get angry.
But, what you've done is very serious.

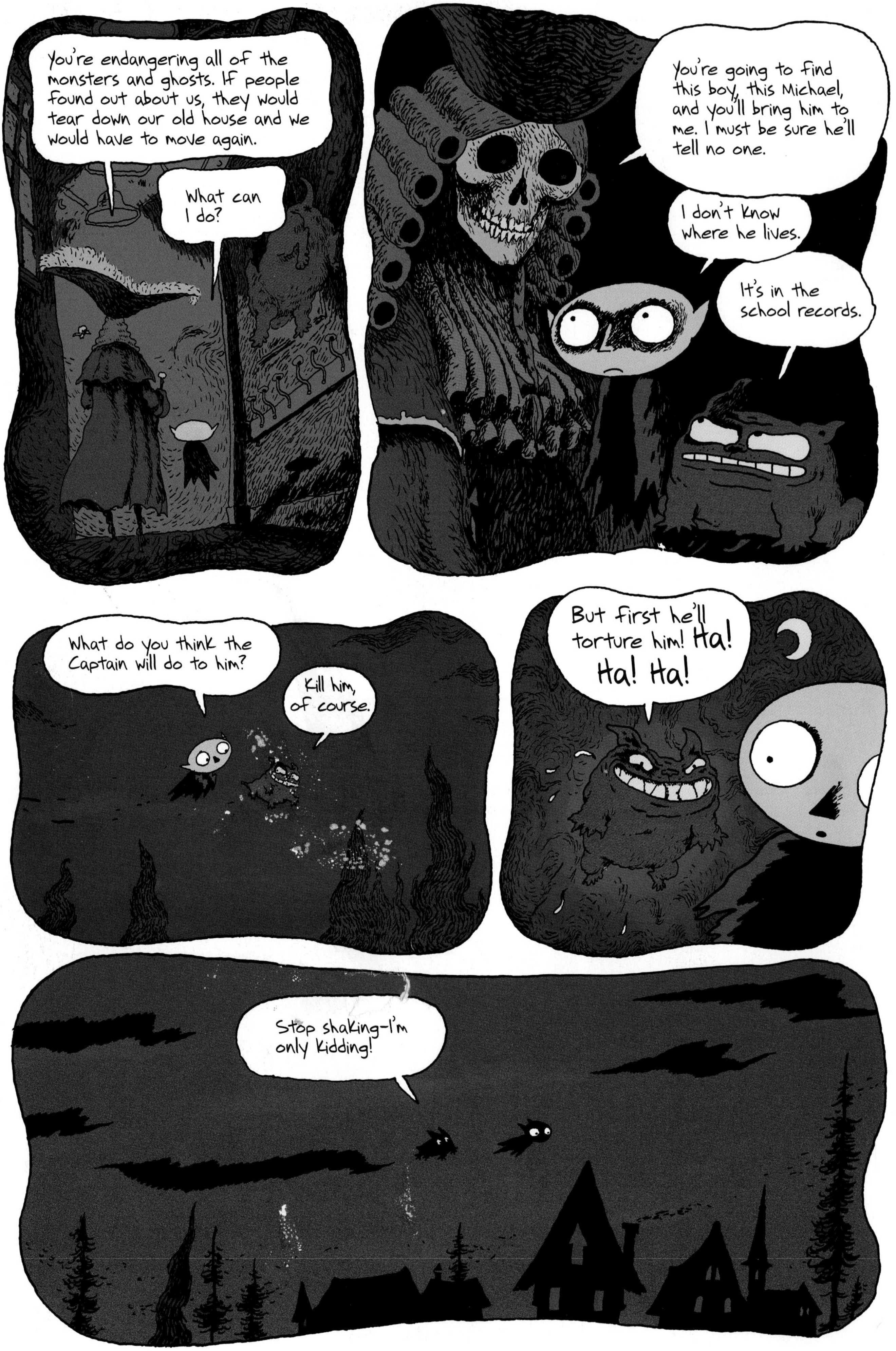
You're endangering all of the monsters and ghosts. If people found out about us, they would tear down our old house and we would have to move again.
What can I do?
You're going to find this boy, this Michael, and you'll bring him to me. I must be sure he'll tell no one.
I don't know where he lives.
It's in the school records.
What do you think the Captain will do to him?
Kill him, of course.
But first he'll torture him! Ha! Ha! Ha!
Stop shaking—I'm only kidding!

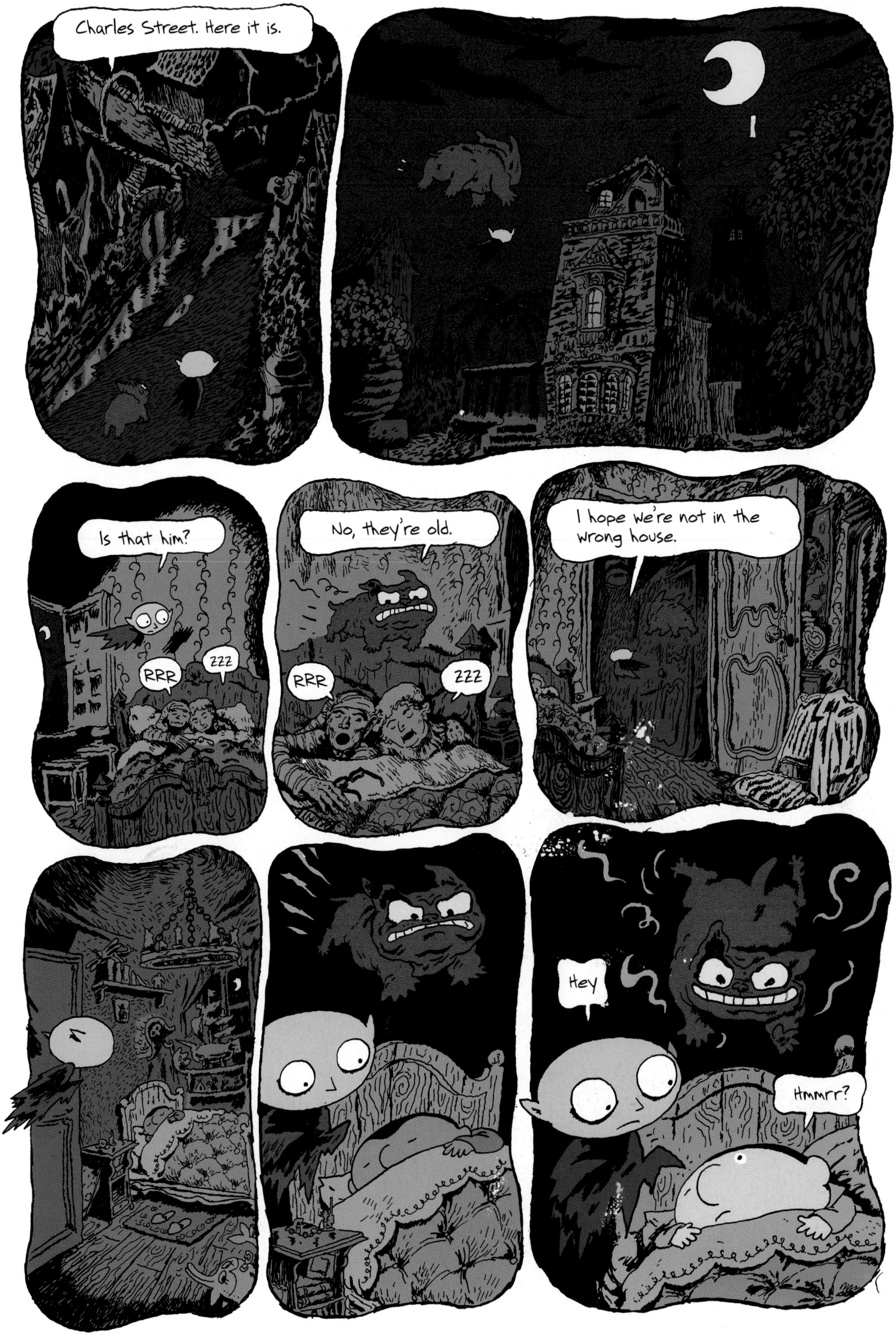

Charles Street. Here it is.
Is that him?
RRR
ZZZ
No, they're old.
RRR
ZZZ
I hope we're not in the wrong house.
Hey
Hmmrr?

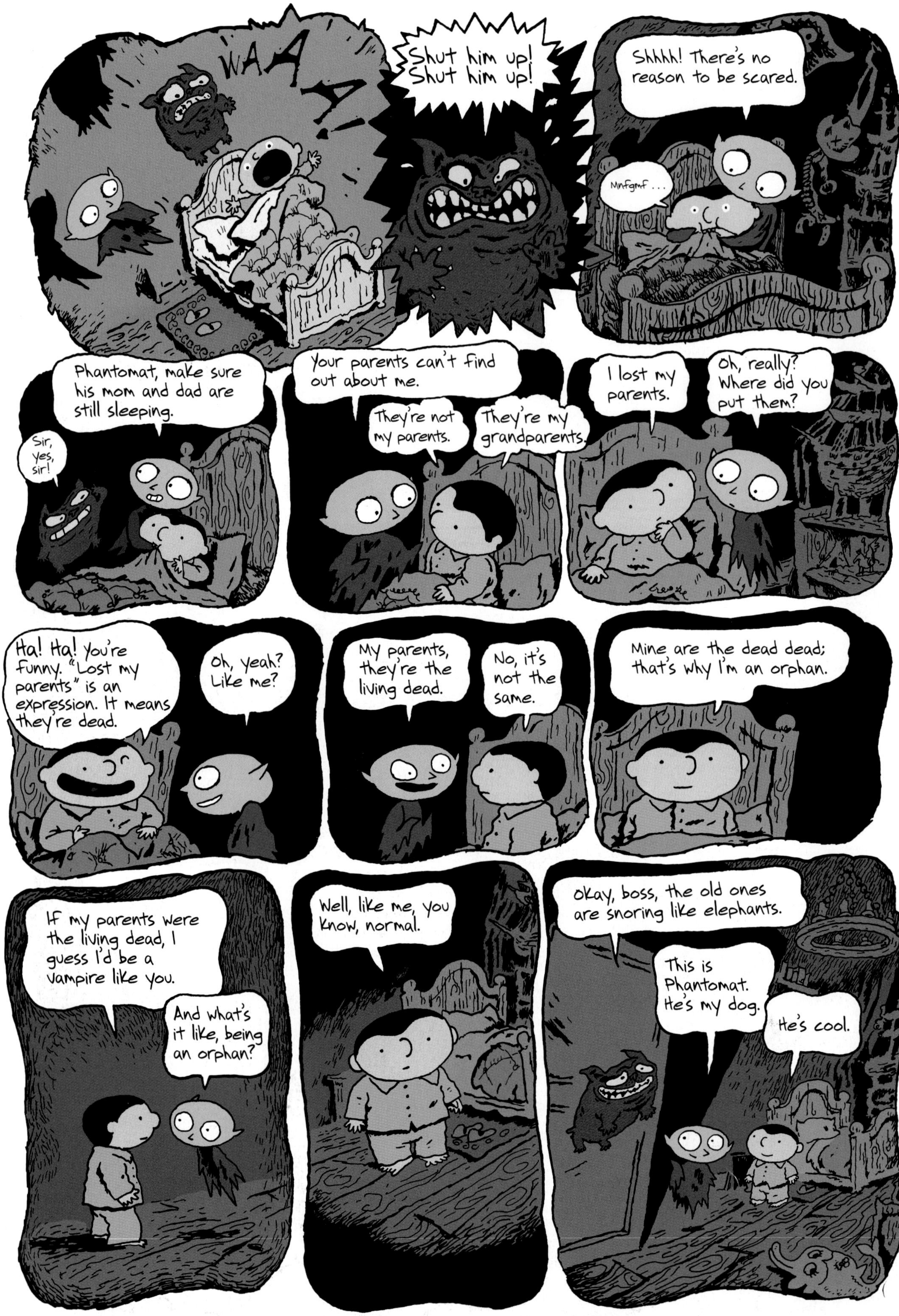
WAAAA!
Shut him up! Shut him up!
Shhhh! There's no reason to be scared.
Mnfgmf . . .
Phantomat, make sure his mom and dad are still sleeping.
Sir, yes, sir!
Your parents can't find out about me.
They're not my parents.
They're my grandparents.
I lost my parents.
Oh, really? Where did you put them?
Ha! Ha! You're funny. "Lost my parents" is an expression. It means they're dead.
Oh, yeah? Like me?
My parents, they're the living dead.
No, it's not the same.
Mine are the dead dead; that's why I'm an orphan.
If my parents were the living dead, I guess I'd be a vampire like you.
And what's it like, being an orphan?
Well, like me, you know, normal.
Okay, boss, the old ones are snoring like elephants.
This is Phantomat. He's my dog.
He's cool.

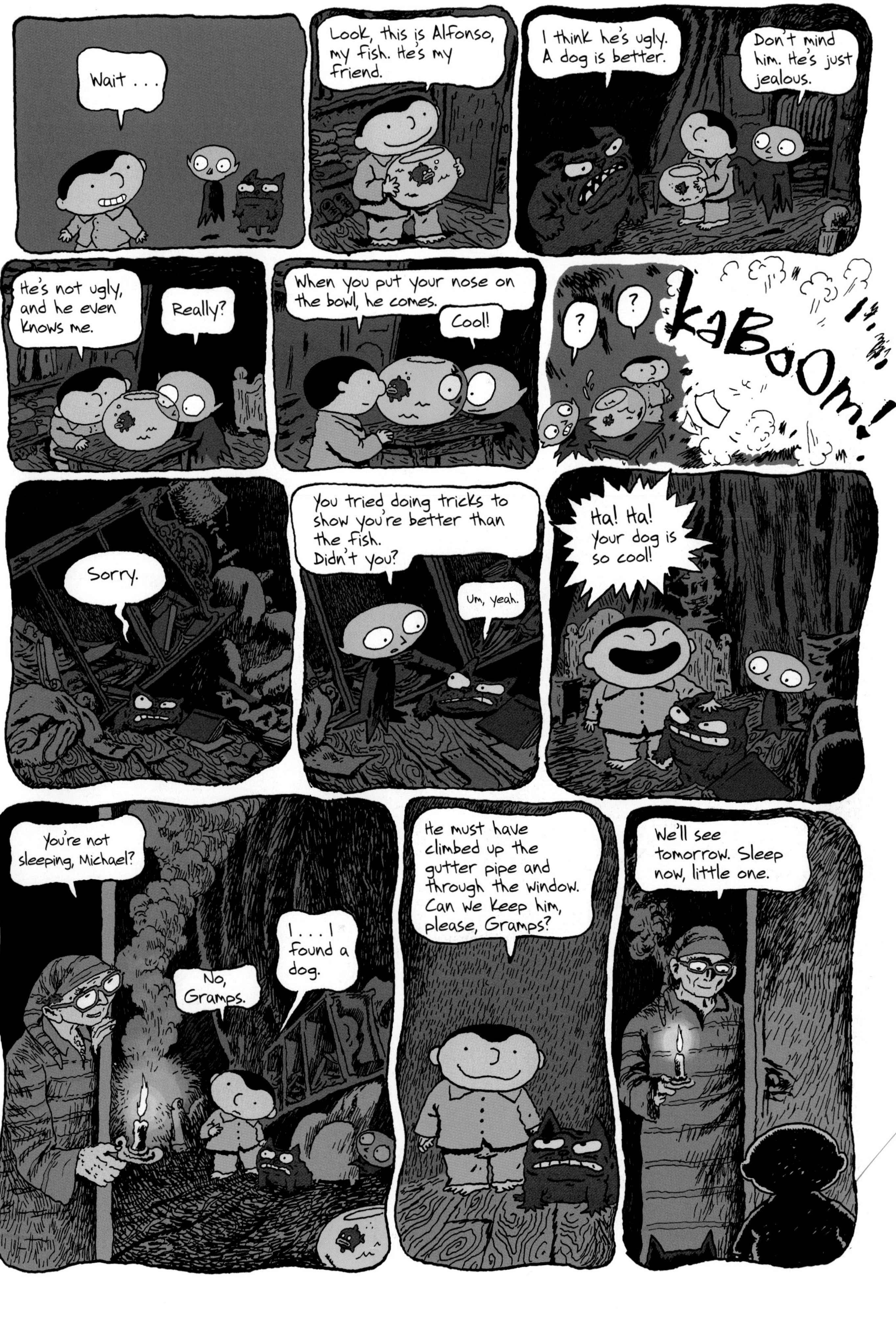
Wait . . .
Look, this is Alfonso, my fish. He's my friend.
I think he's ugly. A dog is better.
Don't mind him. He's just jealous.
He's not ugly, and he even knows me.
Really?
When you put your nose on the bowl, he comes.
Cool!
?
?
KABOOM!
Sorry.
You tried doing tricks to show you're better than the fish. Didn't you?
Um, yeah.
Ha! Ha! Your dog is so cool!
You're not sleeping, Michael?
No, Gramps.
I . . . I found a dog.
He must have climbed up the gutter pipe and through the window. Can we keep him, please, Gramps?
We'll see tomorrow. Sleep now, little one.

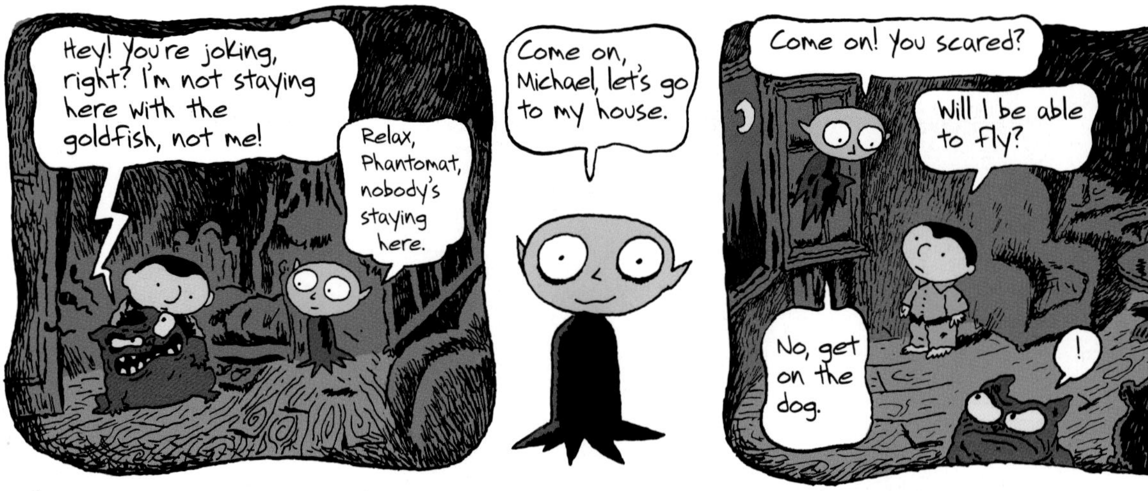
Hey! You're joking, right? I'm not staying here with the goldfish, not me!
Relax, Phantomat, nobody's staying here.
Come on, Michael, let's go to my house.
Come on! You scared?
Will I be able to fly?
No, get on the dog.
!

(Don't do this at home. If your dog isn't magical, you shouldn't climb on him.)

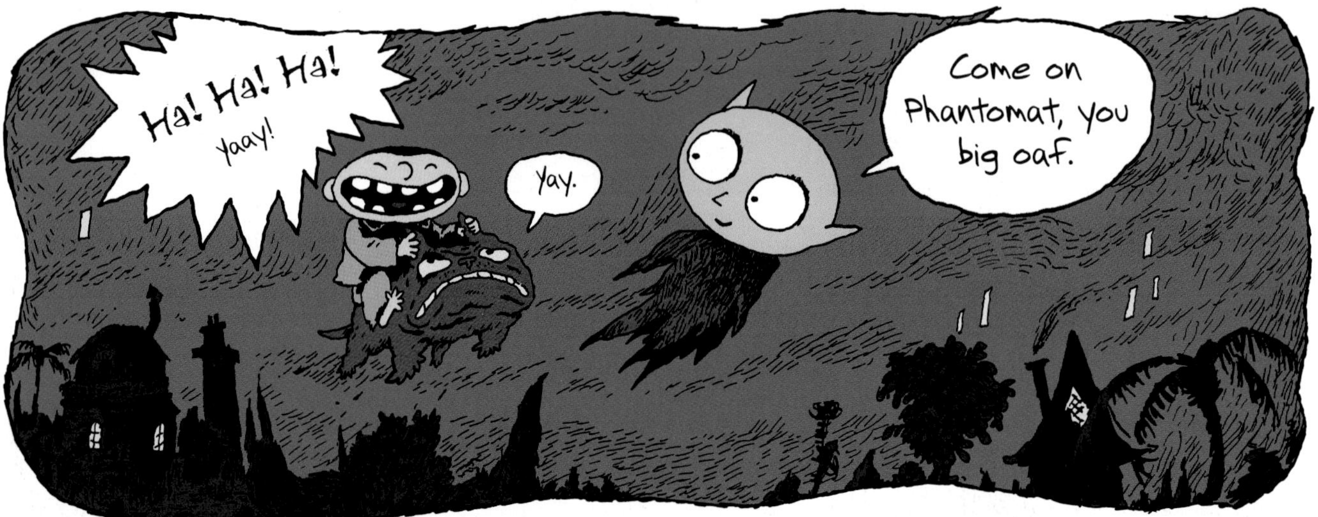
Ha! Ha! Ha!
Yaay!
Yay.
Come on Phantomat, you big oaf.

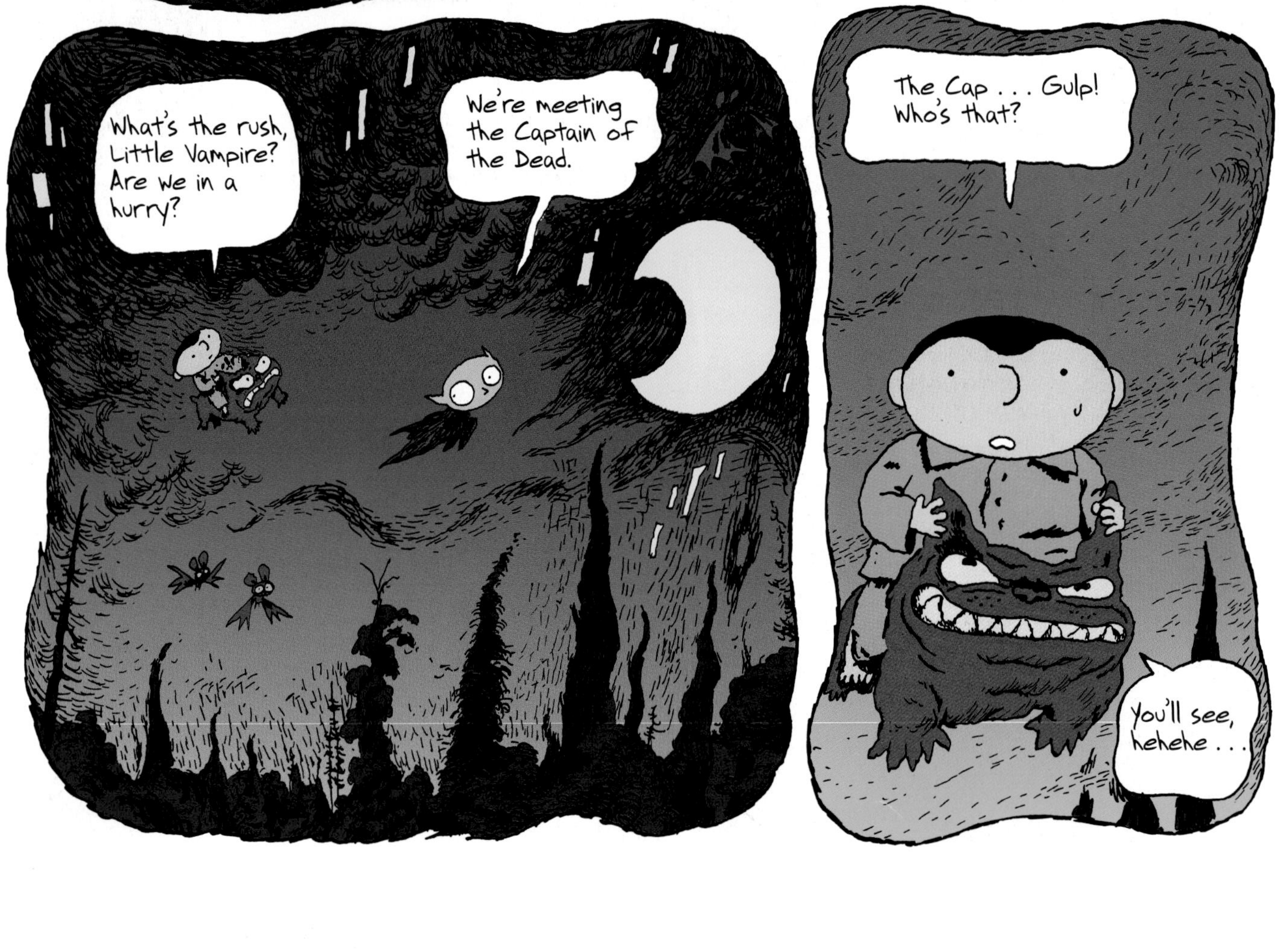
What's the rush, Little Vampire? Are we in a hurry?
We're meeting the Captain of the Dead.
The Cap . . . Gulp! Who's that?
You'll see, hehehe . . .

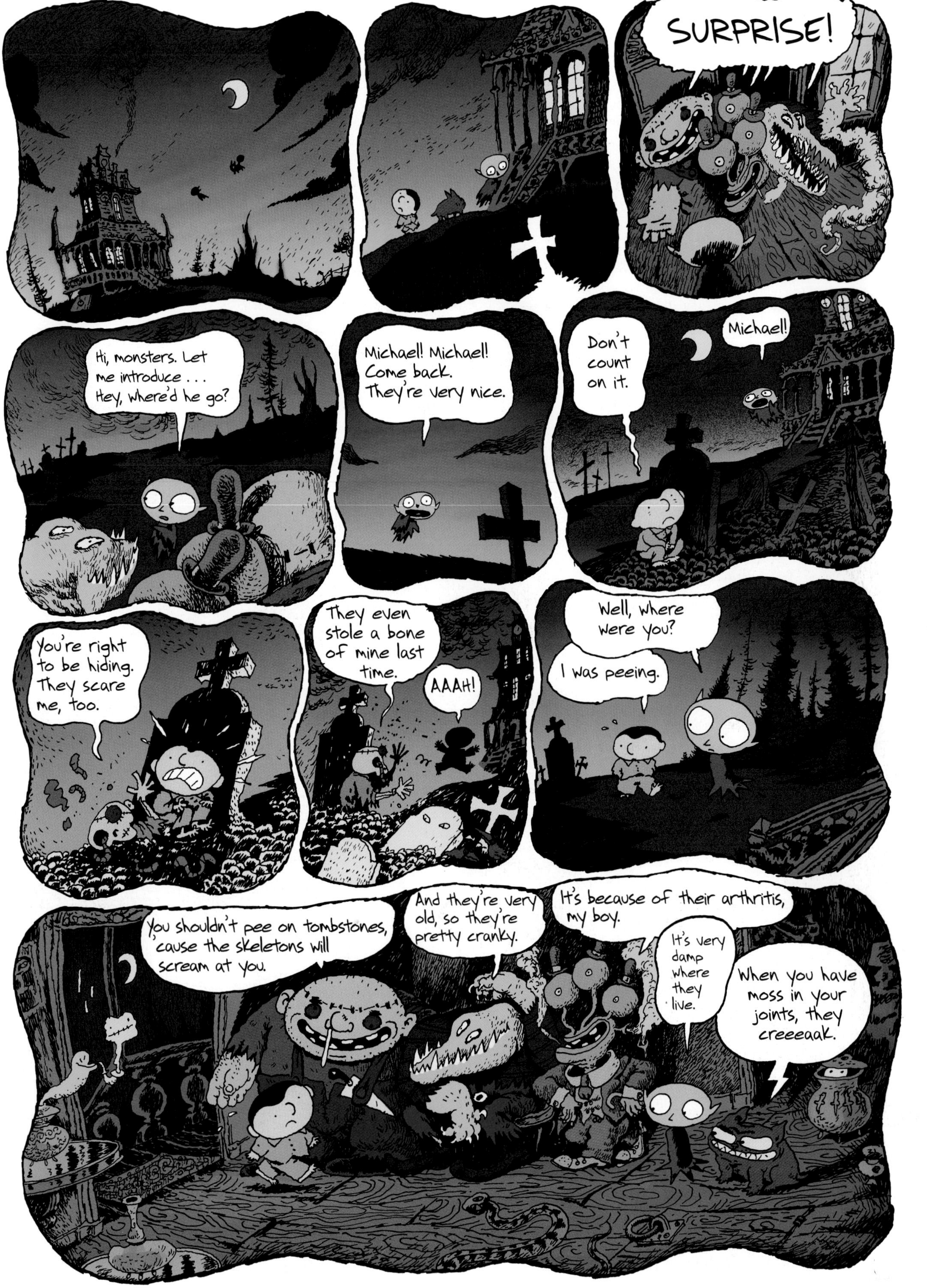
SURPRISE!
Hi, monsters. Let me introduce . . . Hey, where'd he go?
Michael! Michael! Come back. They're very nice.
Michael!
Don't count on it.
You're right to be hiding. They scare me, too.
They even stole a bone of mine last time.
AAAH!
Well, where were you?
I was peeing.
You shouldn't pee on tombstones, 'cause the skeletons will scream at you.
And they're very old, so they're pretty cranky.
It's because of their arthritis, my boy.
It's very damp where they live.
When you have moss in your joints, they creeeaak.

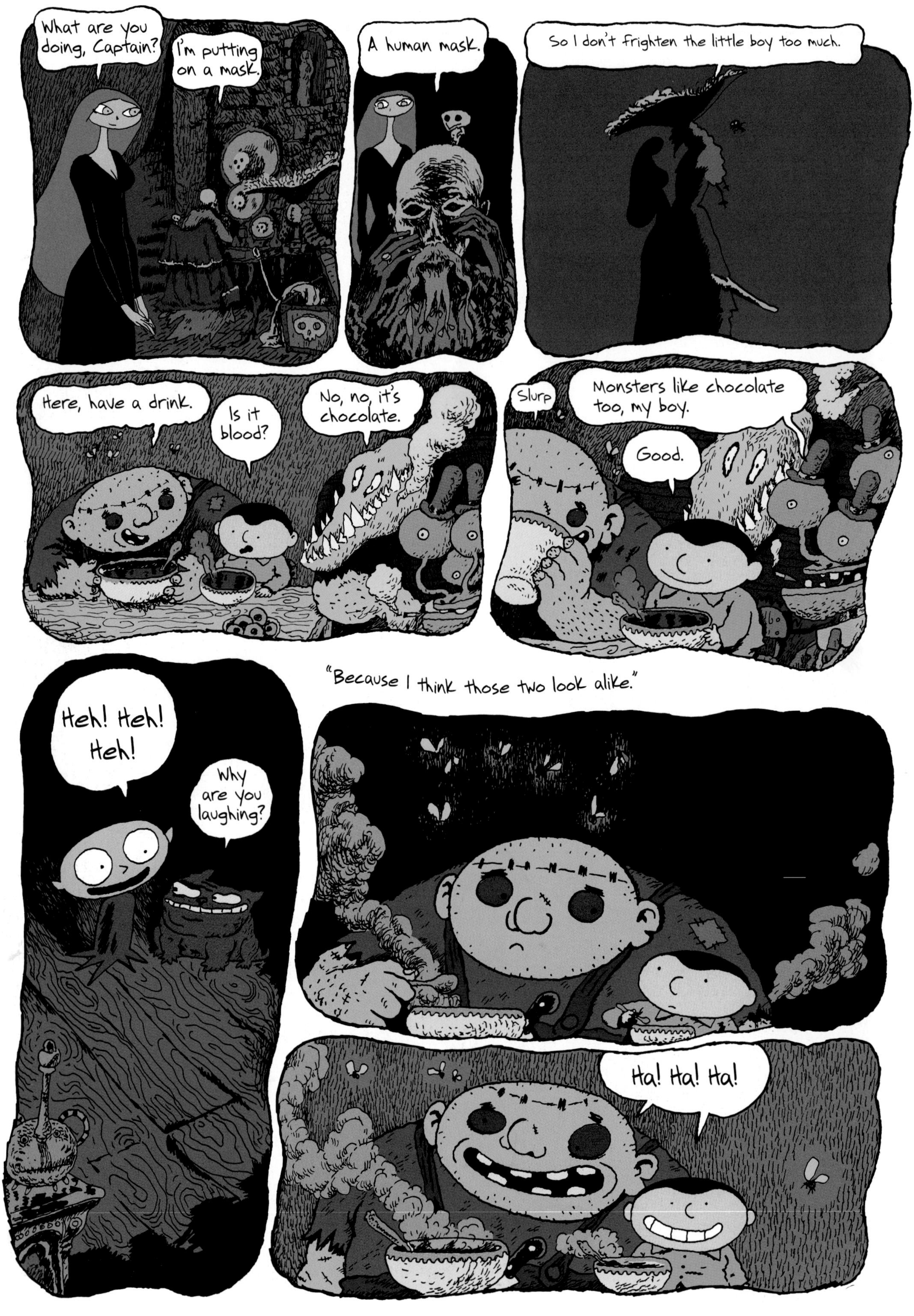
What are you doing, Captain?
I'm putting on a mask.
A human mask.
So I don't frighten the little boy too much.
Here, have a drink.
Is it blood?
No, no, it's chocolate.
Slurp
Monsters like chocolate too, my boy.
Good.
"Because I think those two look alike."
Heh! Heh! Heh!
Why are you laughing?
Ha! Ha! Ha!

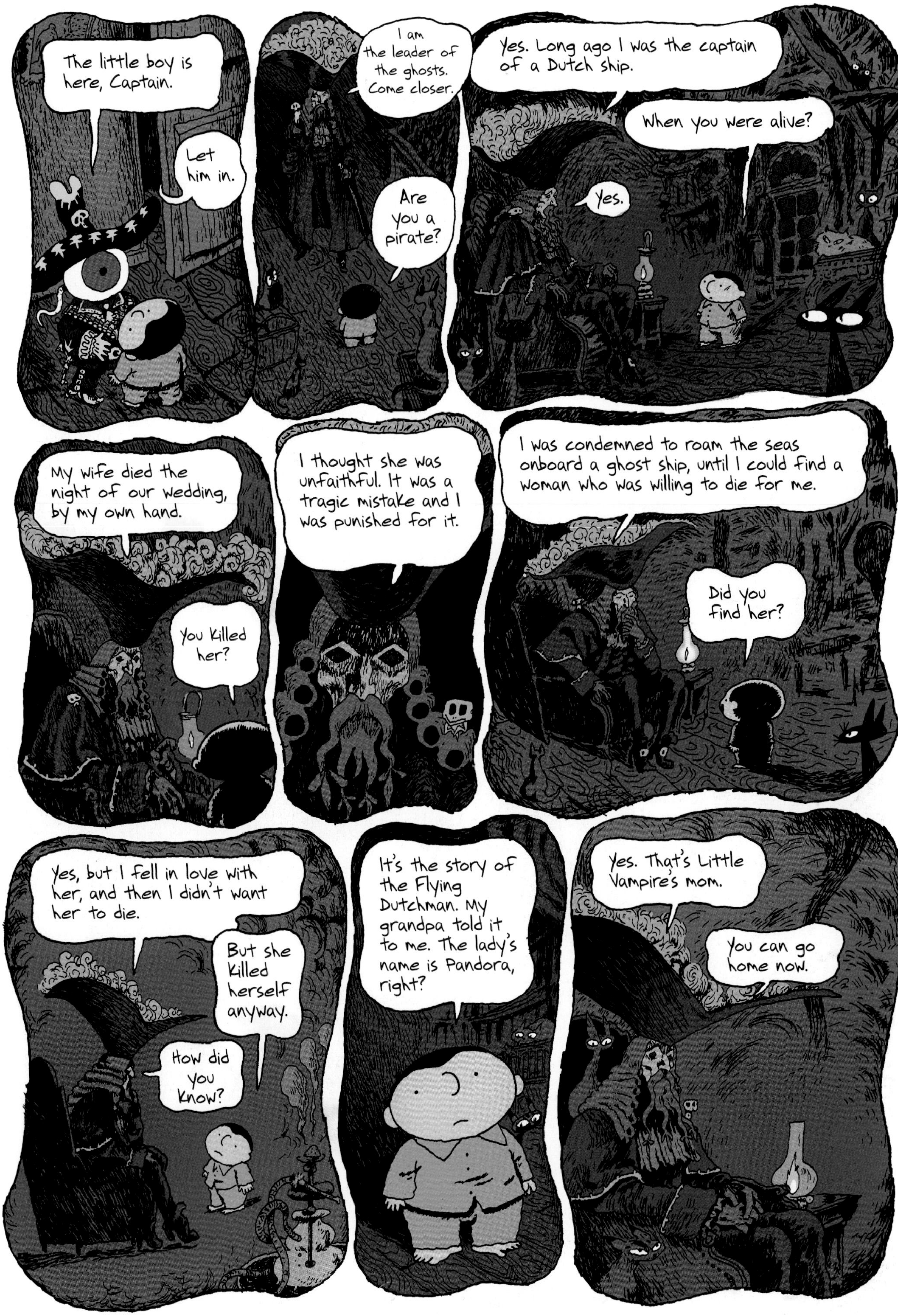
The little boy is here, Captain.
Let him in.
I am the leader of the ghosts. Come closer.
Are you a pirate?
Yes. Long ago I was the captain of a Dutch ship.
When you were alive?
Yes.
My wife died the night of our wedding, by my own hand.
You killed her?
I thought she was unfaithful. It was a tragic mistake and I was punished for it.
I was condemned to roam the seas onboard a ghost ship, until I could find a woman who was willing to die for me.
Did you find her?
Yes, but I fell in love with her, and then I didn't want her to die.
But she killed herself anyway.
How did you know?
It's the story of the Flying Dutchman. My grandpa told it to me. The lady's name is Pandora, right?
Yes. That's Little Vampire's mom.
You can go home now.

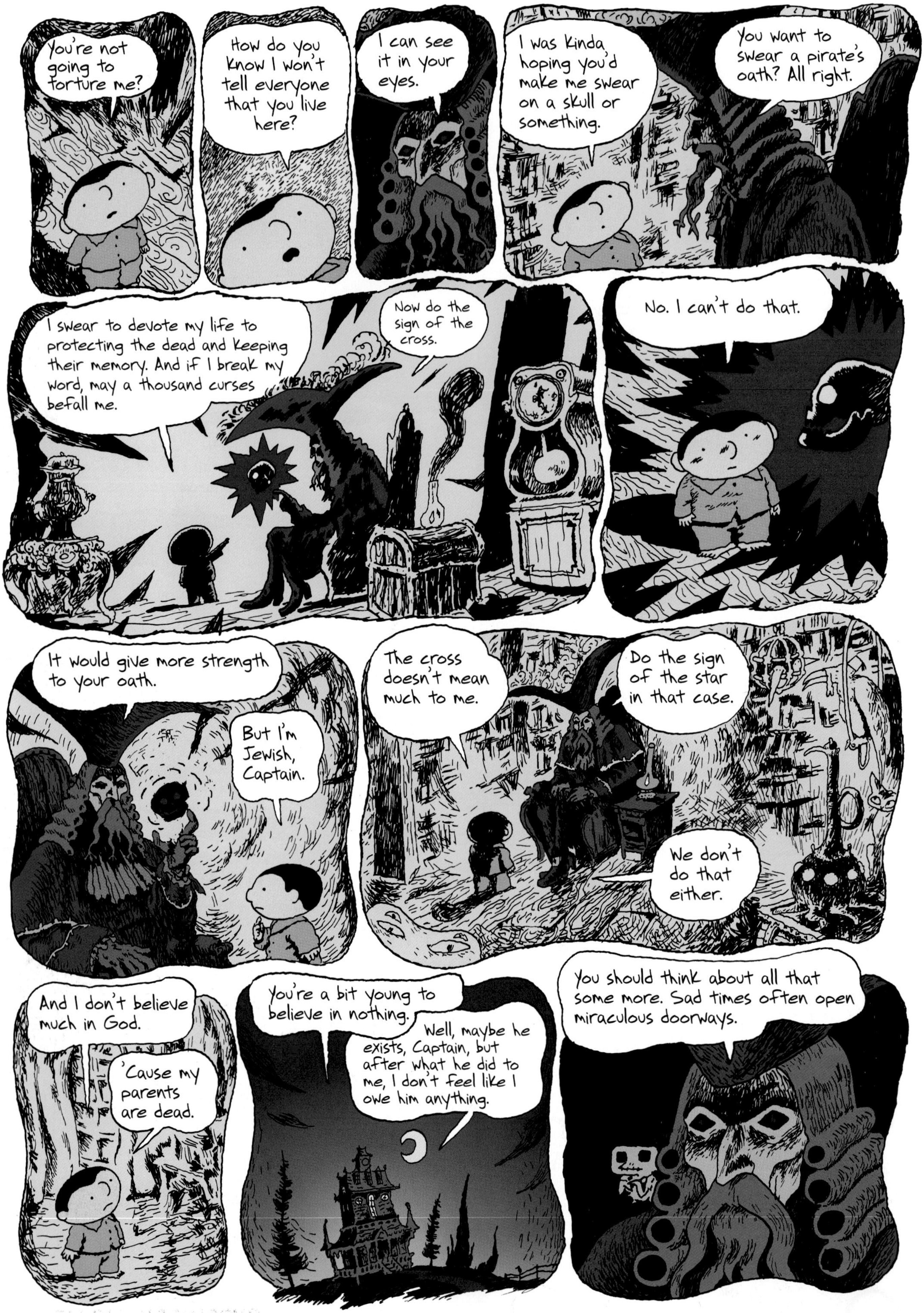
You're not going to torture me?
How do you know I won't tell everyone that you live here?
I can see it in your eyes.
I was kinda hoping you'd make me swear on a skull or something.
You want to swear a pirate's oath? All right.
I swear to devote my life to protecting the dead and keeping their memory. And if I break my word, may a thousand curses befall me.
Now do the sign of the cross.
No. I can't do that.
It would give more strength to your oath.
But I'm Jewish, Captain.
The cross doesn't mean much to me.
Do the sign of the star in that case.
We don't do that either.
And I don't believe much in God.
'Cause my parents are dead.
You're a bit young to believe in nothing.
Well, maybe he exists, Captain, but after what he did to me, I don't feel like I owe him anything.
You should think about all that some more. Sad times often open miraculous doorways.

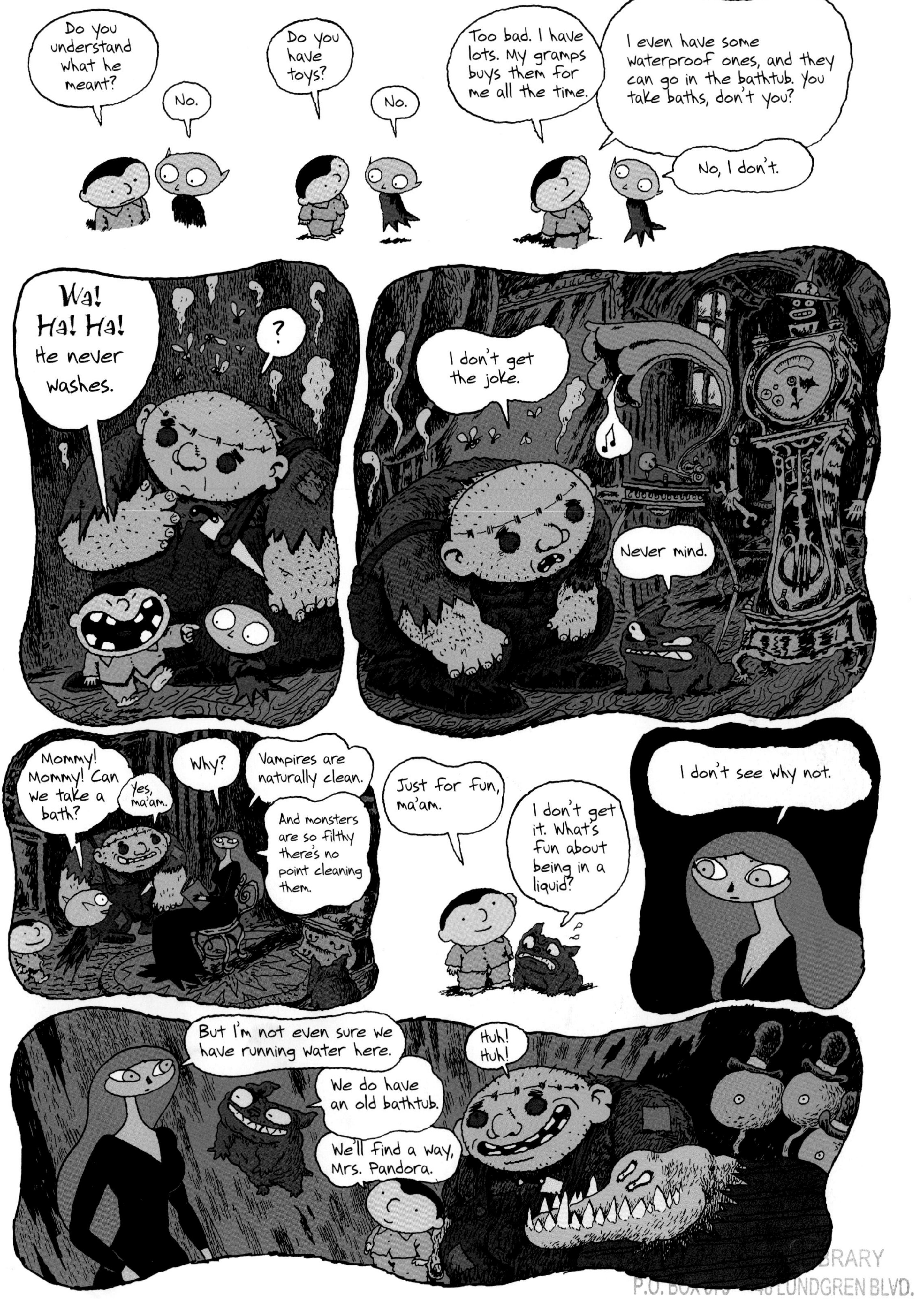
Do you understand what he meant?
No.
Do you have toys?
No.
Too bad. I have lots. My gramps buys them for me all the time.
I even have some waterproof ones, and they can go in the bathtub. You take baths, don't you?
No, I don't.
Wa! Ha! Ha! He never washes.
?
I don't get the joke.
Never mind.
Mommy! Mommy! Can we take a bath?
Yes, ma'am.
Why?
Vampires are naturally clean.
And monsters are so filthy there's no point cleaning them.
Just for fun, ma'am.
I don't get it. What's fun about being in a liquid?
I don't see why not.
But I'm not even sure we have running water here.
Huh! Huh!
We do have an old bathtub.
We'll find a way, Mrs. Pandora.

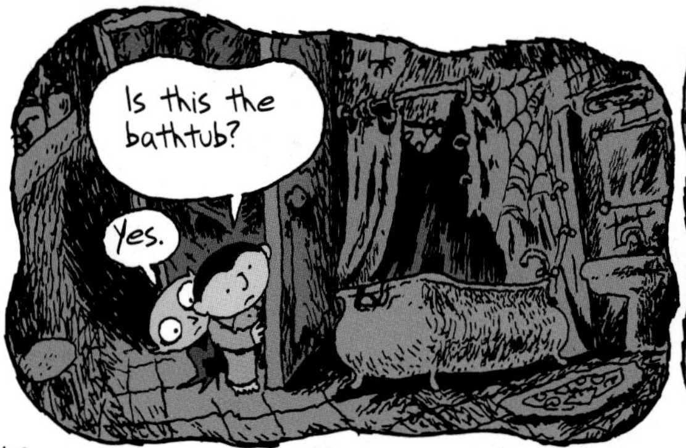
Is this the bathtub?
Yes.

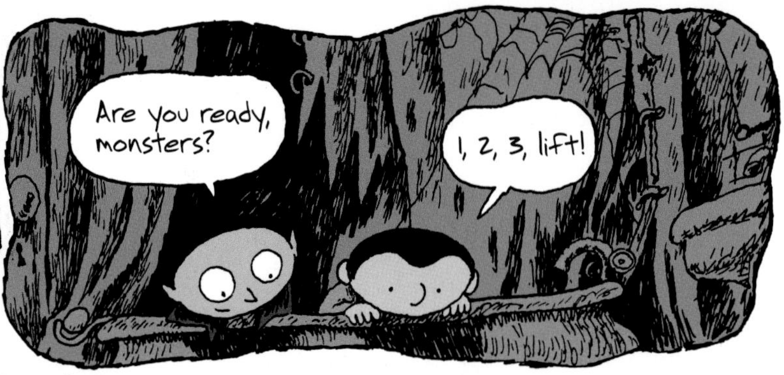
Are you ready, monsters?
1, 2, 3, lift!

The monsters ran off toward the swamp, carrying the bathtub with Little Vampire, Michael, and Phantomat.

Once there, it was easy to fill the tub with mud.

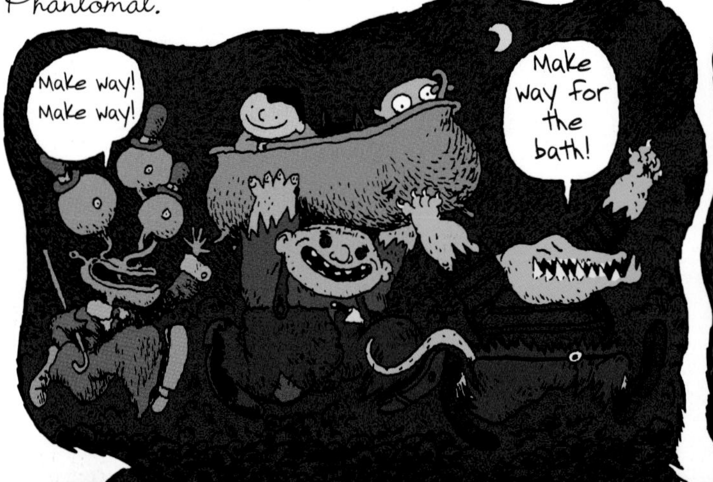
Make way! Make way!
Make way for the bath!

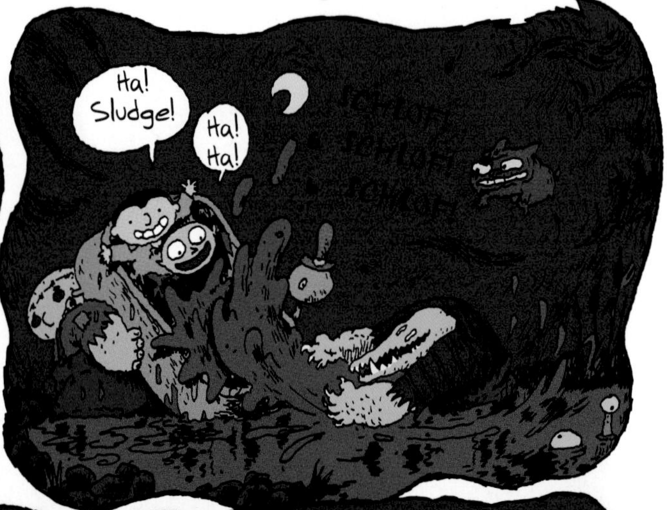
Ha! Sludge!
Ha! Ha!

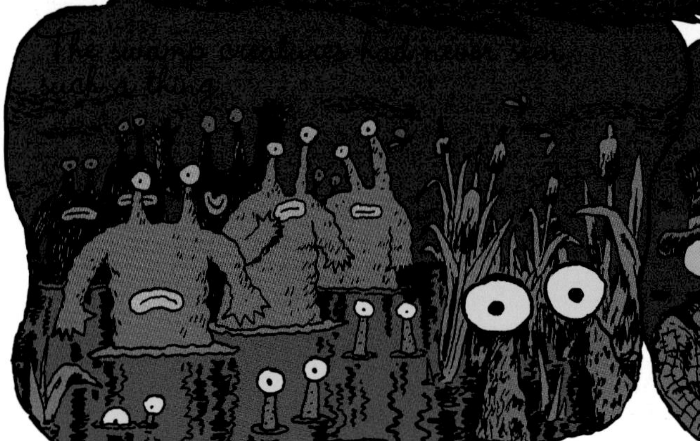

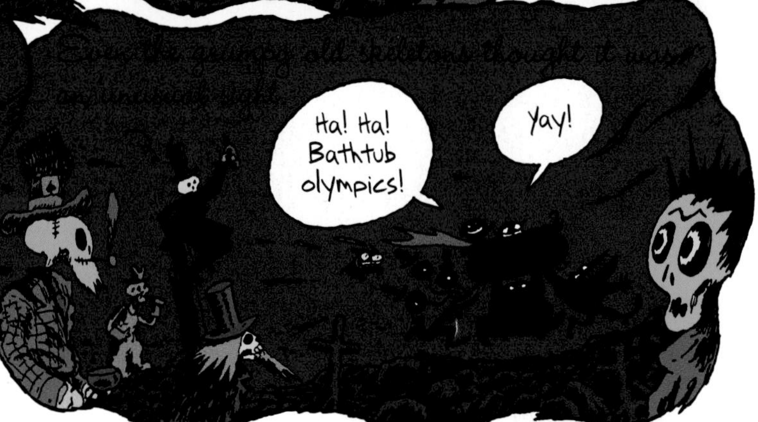
Ha! Ha! Bathtub olympics!
Yay!

When the monsters put down the old tub on the oak table in the living room, all the monsters came to see the bath.

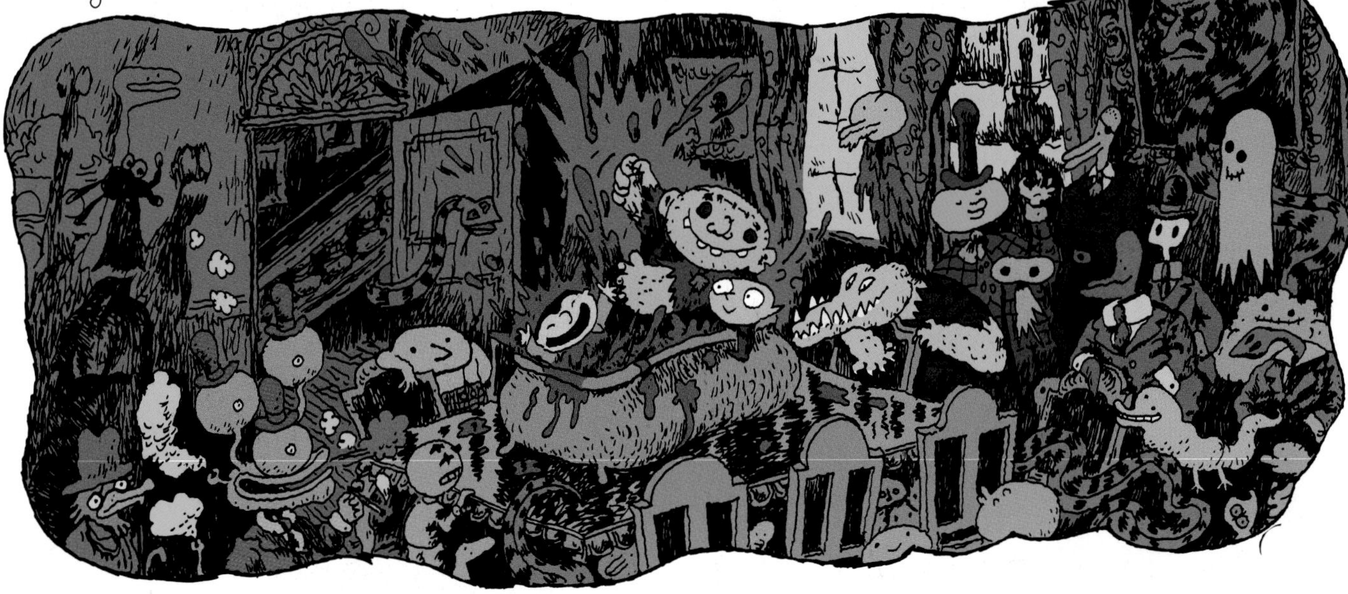

Phantomat didn't like the idea of a bath, but he wasn't given much choice.

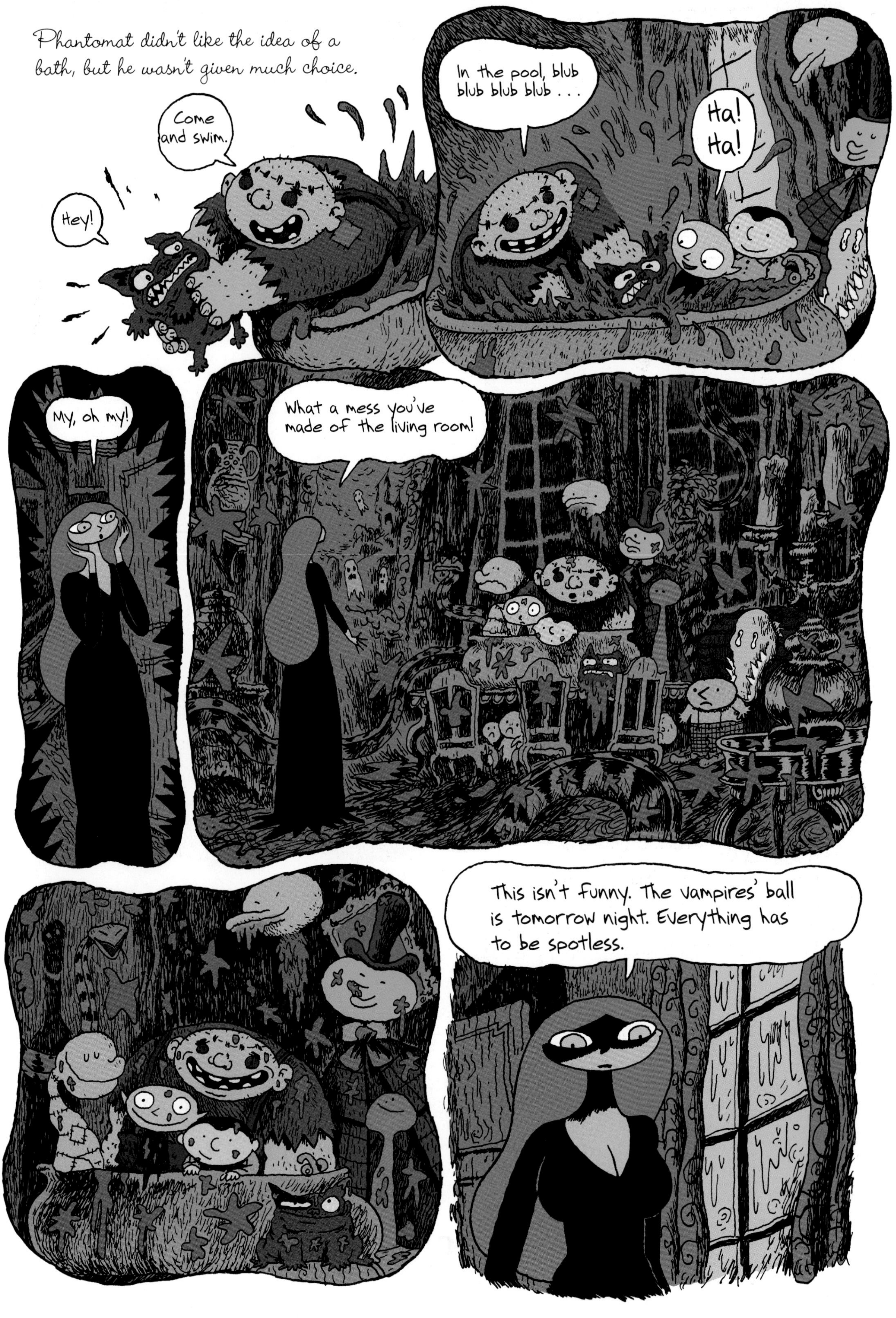

Come and swim.
Hey!
In the pool, blub blub blub blub . . .
Ha! Ha!
My, oh my!
What a mess you've made of the living room!
This isn't funny. The vampires' ball is tomorrow night. Everything has to be spotless.

So everyone spent the rest of the night cleaning the dining room in the old house, so Mrs. Pandora wouldn't be upset. The monsters cleaned like crazy. One or two of them even licked the walls and said mud was tasty. But Michael cleaned with great care, because he was afraid he wouldn't be invited back again to Little Vampire's home if the mess wasn't completely cleaned up.

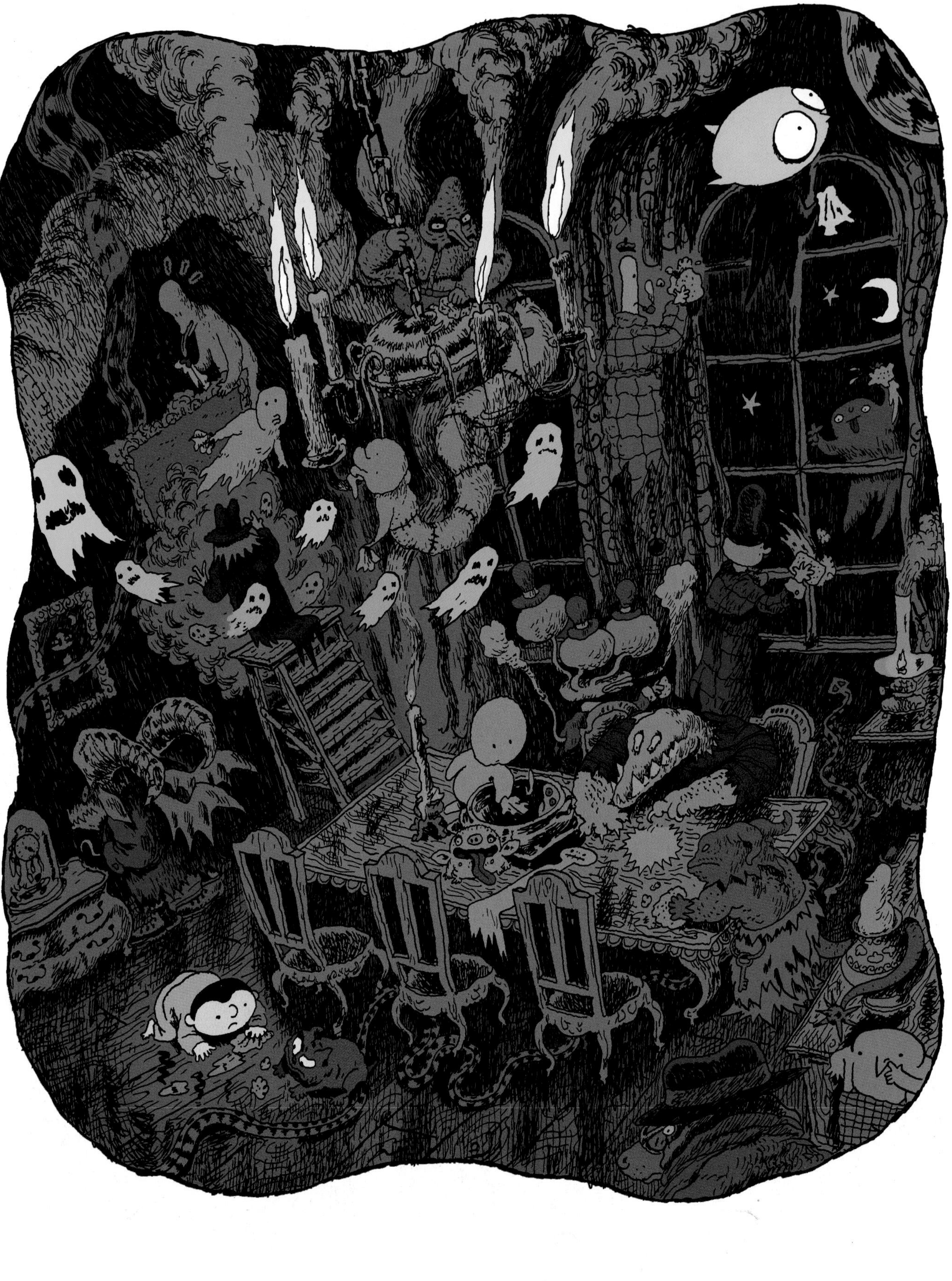

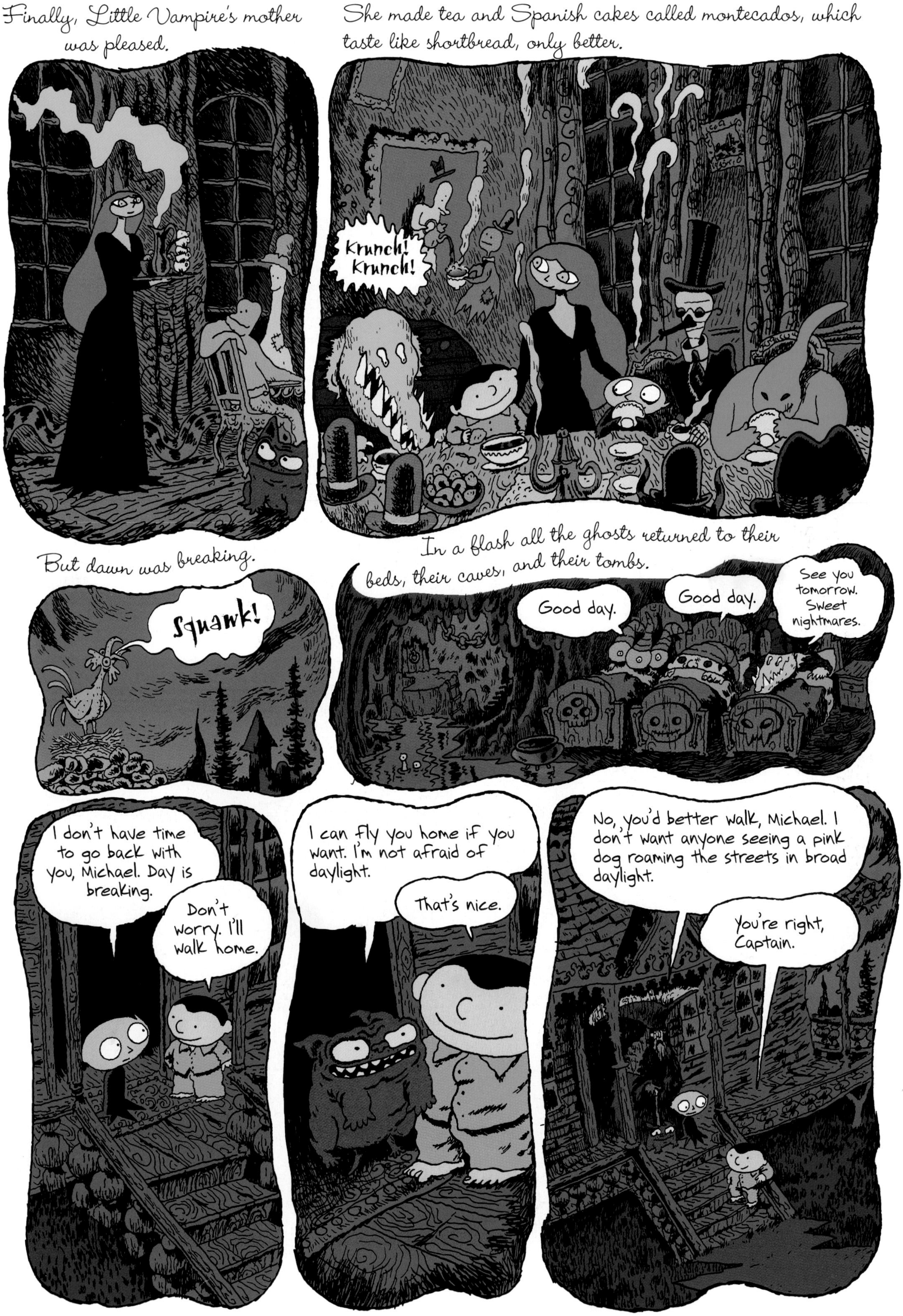
Finally, Little Vampire's mother was pleased.
She made tea and Spanish cakes called montecados, which taste like shortbread, only better.
Krunch! Krunch!
But dawn was breaking.
Squawk!
In a flash all the ghosts returned to their beds, their caves, and their tombs.
Good day.
Good day.
See you tomorrow. Sweet nightmares.
I don't have time to go back with you, Michael. Day is breaking.
Don't worry. I'll walk home.
I can fly you home if you want. I'm not afraid of daylight.
That's nice.
No, you'd better walk, Michael. I don't want anyone seeing a pink dog roaming the streets in broad daylight.
You're right, Captain.

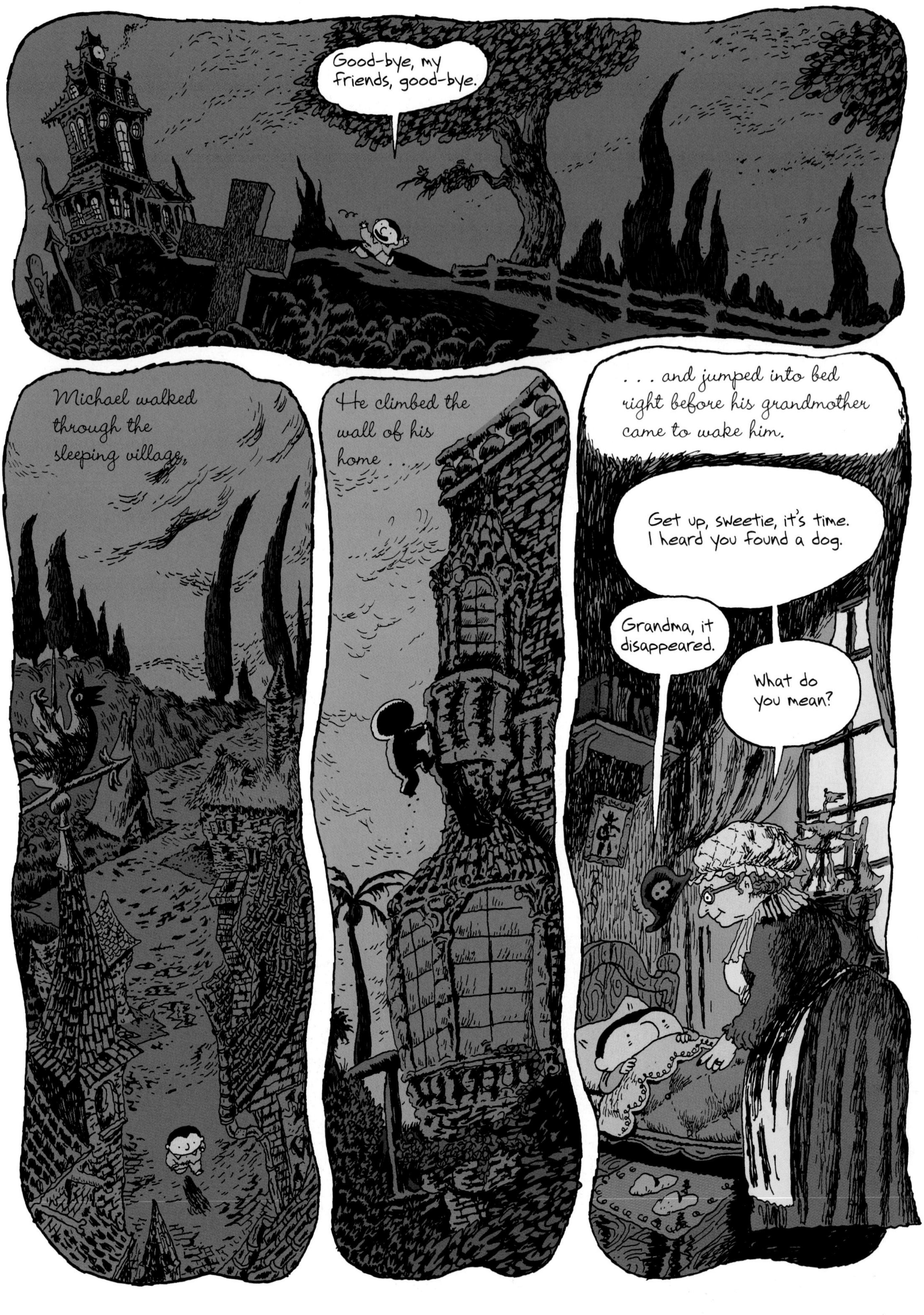
Good-bye, my friends, good-bye.
Michael walked through the sleeping village,
He climbed the wall of his home . . .
. . . and jumped into bed right before his grandmother came to wake him.
Get up, sweetie, it's time. I heard you found a dog.
Grandma, it disappeared.
What do you mean?

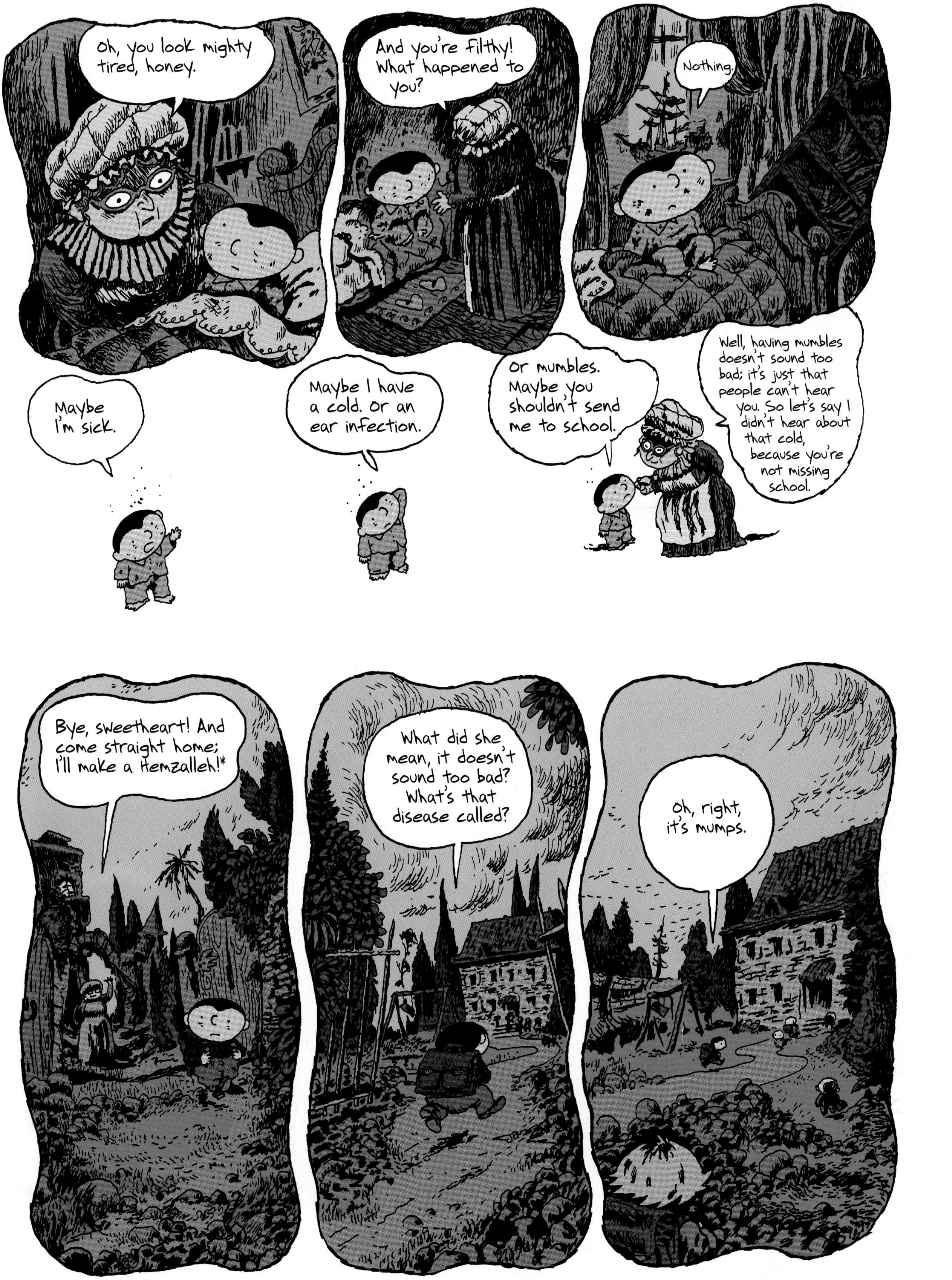
Oh, you look mighty tired, honey.
And you're filthy! What happened to you?
Nothing.
Maybe I'm sick.
Maybe I have a cold. Or an ear infection.
Or mumbles. Maybe you shouldn't send me to school.
Well, having mumbles doesn't sound too bad; it's just that people can't hear you. So let's say I didn't hear about that cold, because you're not missing school.
Bye, sweetheart! And come straight home; I'll make a Hemzalleh!*
What did she mean, it doesn't sound too bad? What's that disease called?
Oh, right, it's mumps.

*Trust me, it's really yummy; you would have to have a grandma like mine to understand.

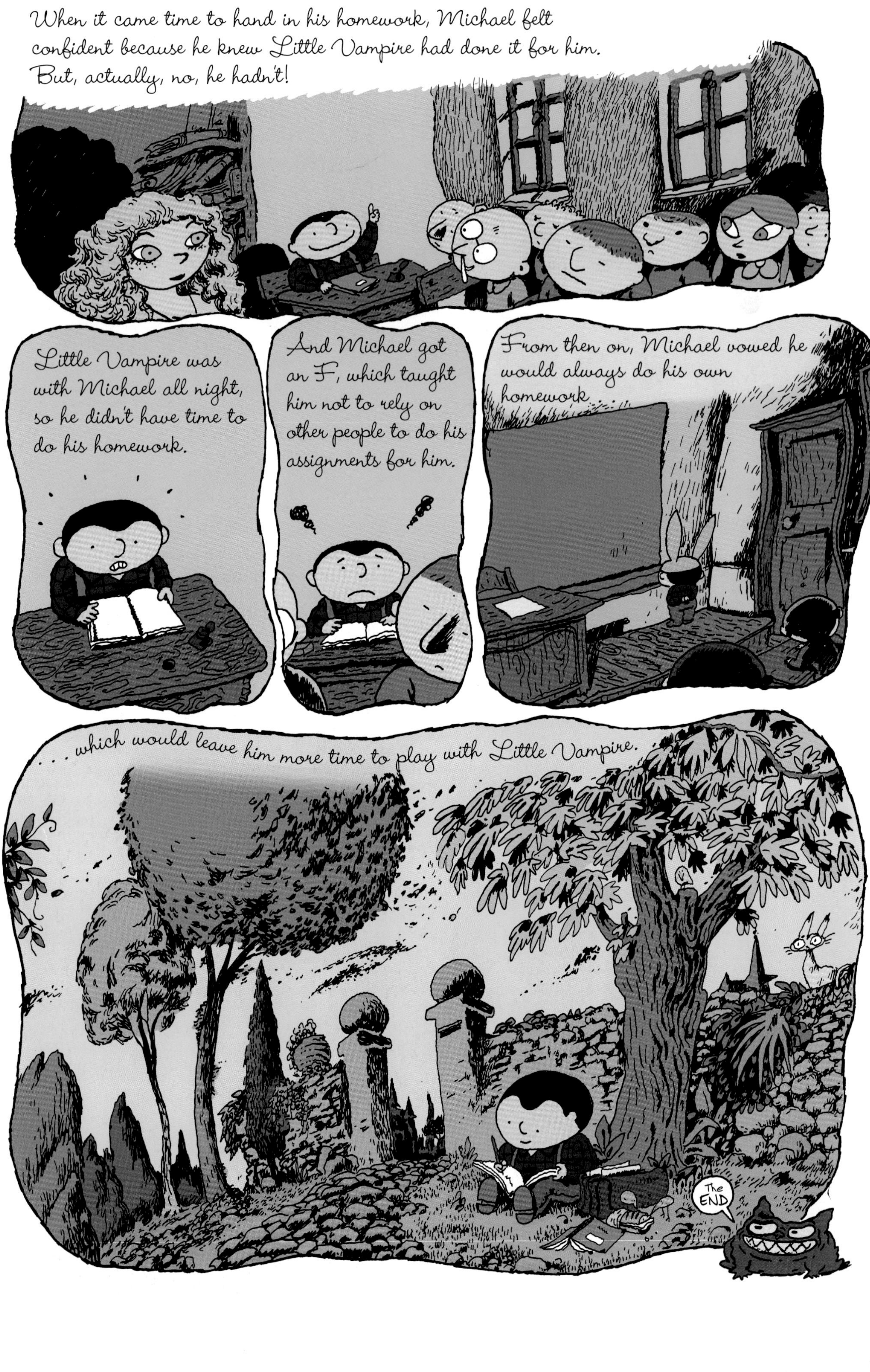
When it came time to hand in his homework, Michael felt confident because he knew Little Vampire had done it for him. But, actually, no, he hadn't!
Little Vampire was with Michael all night, so he didn't have time to do his homework.
And Michael got an F, which taught him not to rely on other people to do his assignments for him.
From then on, Michael vowed he would always do his own homework . . .
. . . which would leave him more time to play with Little Vampire.
The END

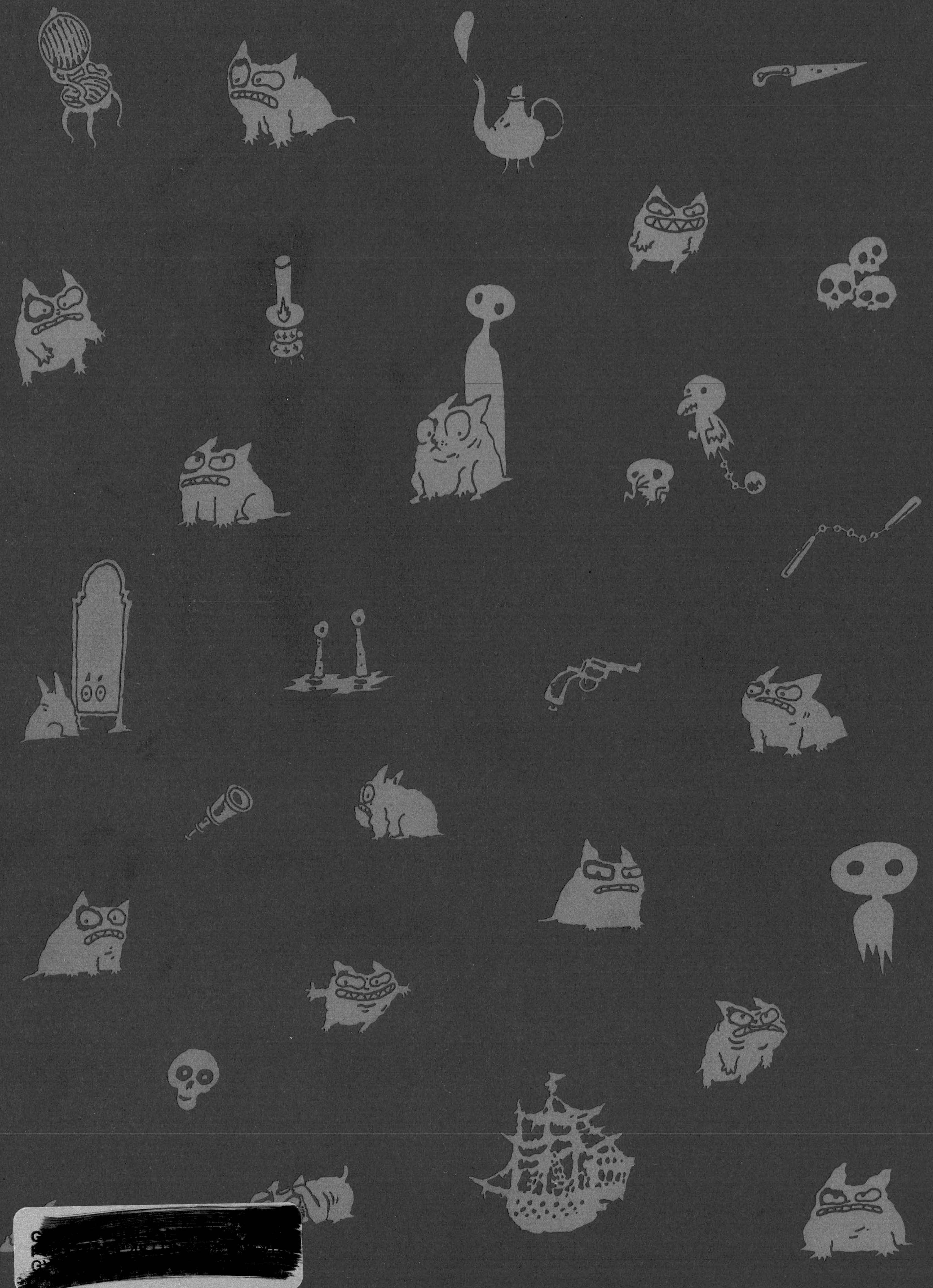

[redacted]